CW00662216

Praise for *Notes on my Family*

"Exceptional YA/adult crossover debut. Narrative voice reminiscent of Mark Haddon or Harper Lee"—Nicolette Jones, Sunday Times Book of the Week

"Masterly"—Oliver Harris

"Warm, witty, moving"—Anna James

The Tiny Gestures of Small Flowers

Emily Critchley

Published in the UK by Everything with Words Limited
Fifth Floor, 30–31 Furnival Street, London, EC4A 1JQ

www.everythingwithwords.com

Text copyright © Emily Critchley 2021
Cover design and illustration by
Holly Ovenden © Everything with Words

A CIP catalogue record for this book is available
from the British Library.

ISBN 978-1-911427-09-4

Printed and bound in Great Britain by
CPI Group (UK) Ltd, Croydon CRO 4YY

To write just one poem you must see many cities, people and things. You must know animals, be able to feel how birds fly and know the gestures which small flowers make when they open in the morning. You must be able to recall roads in unfamiliar places, surprise meetings, partings you knew would happen as well as days of childhood that are still unexplained.

The Notebooks of Malte Laurids Brigge.

Rainer Maria Rilke

Prologue

1985

Alice wakes alone and naked in a loft bedroom somewhere in Camden. She can see a tree branch through the unadorned skylight. It's windy and the branch is swaying slightly, threatening to tap against the glass. The sound of traffic outside reminds her she is somewhere close to the High Street but she can't remember where exactly. Her head feels fuzzy, her mouth dry. She attempts to sit up, shivering a little and pulling the duvet around herself. There is a glass of water on the table next to the bed. Alice reaches for it and takes a few sips, unsure as to how long the water has been there and if it was meant for her.

She allows herself a proper look around the room. It had been too dark last night to take everything in. The room is not what she expected, but then she isn't sure *what* she expected. Something more luxurious? Perhaps something at least a little more grown-up. This room is no different to the kinds of rooms Alice and her student friends rent: small, shabby, barely furnished. It's dim but she can make out an easel in one corner, a desk, a

1

wardrobe, a small basin under the skylight. A well-used toothbrush stands in a dirty glass. The desk is littered with paint palettes, tubes of oil and sticks of charcoal. The wardrobe is painted a strange shade of green. For some reason, Alice thinks of Kandinsky's comment about green being the most anaesthetising colour. A brown tweed jacket has been thrown over the back of an old wooden chair. To the left of the chair is an overflowing laundry basket and at the end of the bed, a portable television set sits on a stand.

Alice replaces the water glass then slides back down under the covers. She places a hand on her abdomen. She feels nauseous. She wishes it could still be yesterday afternoon.

She hears a creaking noise, footsteps on the ladder. She sees the top of his head first, those dark curls already streaked with silver. He's wearing a paisley dressing gown in a faded red and blue print with a thick mustard piping. In one hand he carries a tray holding a cafetière and two glass coffee cups. She watches as he uses his other hand to steady himself on the ladder. The dressing gown is loosely tied, revealing John's chest covered in thick dark hair. She can see the swell of his belly beneath the loose fabric.

He balances the tray on a three-legged stool next to his side of the bed, or the side he slept on last night at least, then takes his glasses from the pocket of his dressing gown and hooks them over his ears. 'I've made coffee.'

'Thank you.' Alice sits up. Remembering she is naked, she clutches at the duvet.

John sits on the bed causing the mattress to dip. He seems not to notice Alice's nakedness although he certainly noticed it last night. She has the terrifying thought that he may want sex again and hopes he doesn't remove his dressing gown.

John pours black coffee into a cup and hands it to her. 'I'm teaching this morning,' he says. 'Otherwise I'd take you for breakfast. The Good Fayre does terrific eggs.'

Alice nods. She stares into the black, steaming liquid and tries not to think about last night. Wasn't this what she'd wanted? Wasn't this what she'd moved to London for? Along with art, of course. Sex? Adventure? Something different? Now here she is lying naked on a worn purple sheet with John Manly acting as if nothing has happened and talking about terrific eggs.

'You can have a shower if you like. Robson's left for work already. There's no one else here.'

She takes a sip of coffee. It's comforting and familiar and she is grateful for it. Still, she does not want to be here, in John's bed, on a Tuesday morning, trying not to roll into the middle because of the uneven weight distribution. She wants, desperately now, to be outside in the cold February air, making her way back to her room where Gail will surely be wondering why Alice didn't come home last night.

'It's okay,' she says quietly. 'I think I'll shower at home.'

John makes no comment on this.

Alice wonders if John will take as much time over her work, if he'll continue to watch her as closely in the classroom now *this* has happened. Perhaps, she thinks, he will be embarrassed to look at her, or perhaps she will become like everyone else, just another student, no longer special. 'You're very talented, Alice,' he had said that first day. She'd felt his hand on her shoulder as she worked, his breath warm in her ear. 'You're the most talented student I've had in a very long time,' he'd told her last week when she'd helped him put the easels away. Yesterday evening, as they'd left the pub, he'd put his arm around her and she'd thought, *if only they could see me now, if only they could see me with John Manly.* Out of everyone, he'd chosen her.

Alice had felt woozy and remembers, now, how she'd giggled as they'd reached the front door of the house, how John had fumbled for his keys. Upstairs, he'd turned the storage heater on then stood behind his easel. 'I've always wanted to draw you, Alice.' She'd felt his eyes on her as she slowly removed her coat, jumper, blouse, skirt, tights and, finally, her underwear.

Once he was satisfied with his sketch, he'd grunted, stepped out from behind the easel and tossed the stick of charcoal onto the desk. He'd removed his clothes and joined her on the bed, his hand reaching for her breast and as he'd entered her, 'Oh, my darling girl. My darling, darling, girl.'

John puts his coffee cup on the tray. He gets up and switches the TV on. 'Let's see what the milk snatcher's up to now.' He fiddles with the aerial. When he's happy with the picture he returns to the bed.

Alice's clothes, coat and boots are on the floor. She slips out of bed and begins to dress, slowly and methodically but without delay. She glances at John to make sure he isn't looking at her. He isn't. His eyes are fixed on the TV.

The sound of the female news reporter's voice fills the silence of the room.

Yesterday morning, at eleven thirty-eight U.S. Eastern Standard Time, the American space shuttle Challenger exploded, killing all seven astronauts on board.

'You heard about this?' John asks.

Alice nods.

'Awful,' he says, reaching for his coffee.

Alice glances at the TV. The space shuttle explodes in a ball of yellow fire. The image makes her feel queasy and she turns away. She finds her satchel and folder and remembers her earrings on the bedside table. She picks them up and begins to put them in. John leans over and pats her thigh affectionately. Alice flinches. The woman on the television is now talking about helicopters and rescue bids.

5

'Don't forget the still-life set up on Thursday,' John tells her. 'I'm relying on you.'

'I'll be there.'

'Want me to walk you down?'

She shakes her head. 'I can let myself out.'

John nods, clearly pleased he doesn't have to get up. He leans back against the pine headboard and scratches his ear.

Alice pauses at the top of the ladder. 'See you Thursday.'

John looks at her and smiles. Alice can feel his eyes taking her in. They move over her blouse, her short corduroy skirt, her legs. John's look is one of knowingness and possession. Alice feels that something deep inside herself has been broken, violated. She is unable to make sense of it. She cannot say she did not agree to the drink with John yesterday. She had wanted it, in fact. Hadn't she hung back, pretending to tidy the paints so she could be the last one in the room?

'See you Thursday,' John says, and then, as if remembering something, 'I had a nice time last night.'

1

2002

Brighton. She doesn't know it at all. She sits in the café in Waterstones drinking a latte. The café is on the top floor and, out of the window, she has a view of the sea and the pier, its end shrouded in mist. The coffee makes her feel shaky. She isn't used to it. Only Alice drinks coffee. On the chair next to Nell is her rucksack containing all that she has brought with her. She watches as the barista in his checked shirt wipes the table opposite, humming to himself. He moves behind the counter, re-arranges the cakes. It's still early in the morning and, apart from the barista, there is no one else in the café, or indeed on the entire floor.

There is something comforting and familiar about bookshops, all that knowledge and experience waiting to be discovered, all those secrets, private and collective pain, joys and triumphs hidden amongst thousands of pages. It's why she's here. She needs somewhere safe to think about what comes next, to reflect on her first night in the city.

When she'd arrived in Brighton yesterday all the shops had looked huge compared to those at home. She'd walked from the station, through the town, straight to the seafront where she had stood, staring at the mass of pale green water, at the foamy waves crashing against the pebbles. The day was drizzly and grey much like today and she found it difficult to tell if the moisture on her face was rain or sea spray. She'd gripped the railing and looked at the pier, blurred by the rain. A teenager with a blue Mohican and a tiny star tattoo on his left cheekbone rolled past her on his skateboard. There was something pleasing about having the city behind her and the vast expanse of flat grey-green water ahead of her; the juxtaposition of the controlled urban environment butting up against nature. She breathed in damp salty air, the taste of freedom. *The sea, the sea.* Isn't that what the roaming Greeks cried when they finally reached it?

The beach below was empty, not how Nell remembered it from that hot summer day all those years ago. She'd curled her fingers around her hag stone in her pocket, taking comfort in its familiar smooth edges. Her phone beeped. It was Alice, of course.

Are you there yet?

Yes.

Let me know where you're staying tonight.

Ok.

8

Nell had crossed the road and entered an American-style diner where she'd ordered a plate of waffles. The portions were large and she couldn't finish her meal. She'd asked the waitress with the nose ring where the youth hostel was. 'Cross at the pier, love. Straight up the road. Keep walking. On the right.'

And so she'd spent the night in a room of six bunk beds. Two of the beds were occupied by German girls, friends travelling together. They'd sat on the opposite bunk poring over a map of London which Nell imagined was where they'd set off for early this morning. She hadn't learned German at school and couldn't understand anything the girls were saying to each other. She had a GCSE in French (grade B) which was as far as she'd got with languages. She'd recently dropped out of her A-levels. She winced whenever she thought of it. Alice's disappointment. But why stay when she could go? Nell had understood, though, when the larger of the German girls shouted *'scheisse!'* after banging her shin coming down the ladder in the morning.

In the bookshop café, Nell takes the piece of crumpled paper from her pocket and lays it on the table, smoothing it out with the palm of her hand. It's a list of names and numbers. She's made notes in the margins: *close to the town centre, furnished, cat, oblique sea view, vegetarian household.*

She makes it clear, on the phone, to those numbers that are answered anyway, that she needs to see the rooms today, if possible, that she's ready to move in. Some of the rooms aren't unavailable until next week, or next month. Too late.

Her fourth call is answered by a girl – Kelly-Ann. 'I'm home from work around six if you want to come over then. Do you have the address?' She can just about make out Kelly-Ann's words over the cacophony of voices, eighties pop music, and what sounds like hairdryers.

Nell finishes the last of her coffee and picks up her rucksack. Her plan for the day is to look in the shop windows for job vacancies. Pete and Sandra from the garage had told her they would happily provide her with a reference. 'Are you kidding? You're the best worker we've had,' Sandra had said. 'Who else reorganises the confectionary on a late shift? Anybody would be lucky to have you.'

She'd enjoyed serving the customers, getting their cigarettes, confirming which pump was theirs, telling them where to insert their card or giving them their change. She found it interesting, the things people decided to buy along with their petrol: dog food, de-icer, tampons, Paracetamol, throat sweets, chocolate, a lottery ticket, tinned tomato soup. The items always said something about the person, or at least the person at that very moment. She'd showed the lorry drivers how to use the temperamental coffee machine. Having spent several hours alone, they were often the most talkative. Twenty-five pounds a day on a Saturday, half that for an evening shift. It had felt like a lot. Once she had broken up from school for the summer, finished her GCSEs, she'd been able to take on more shifts, covering holidays and sickness. As her weeks at the garage passed, she became less diligent about watching every car that pulled into the forecourt, trying to make out the face behind the wheel. It was another reason she wanted to get away. The possibility that Darren might have leave, might walk into the garage, or that she might see him in town one day, made her feel uneasy. Once, when she had been in Tesco with Alice, she was sure it was him at the end of the aisle. She had darted behind Alice until she realised it wasn't Darren at all, just a tall dark-haired boy with a strong jaw line and a slight stoop who was looking at dried pasta.

'What's the matter?' Alice had asked.

'Oh, nothing. I thought I saw a teacher, that's all. Mr Freeman.'

'I'm sure he'd be even less thrilled to see you on a Sunday.'

Nell had pretended to study their shopping list. 'Well, anyway. It wasn't him.'

She exits the bookshop and steps out into the damp morning. A gathering of foreign students with matching rucksacks are standing around the clock-tower. Already, she loves the double decker buses that remind her she is in a city. She loves the people, the shops, and that there are houses on both sides of the road. There are no fields, no cows, no dykes. There is no school and no Alice.

2

Nell spends the day wandering around the city. Along with searching for job vacancy signs, she browses the stalls in the South Lanes looking at hats, scarves, earrings, and leather bags with colourful tassels. The seagulls are as big as turkeys and watch her eagerly as she eats her sandwich from Boots. She sits on the bench in the Pavilion Gardens until it begins to rain, then shelters inside the charity shops.

At five o'clock she sets off, intending to find the address ahead of time. The light is fading. It's a quiet October evening with a chill in the air and a shine to the pavements from the earlier rain.

The cream, terraced townhouse is close to a square, not far from the back of the shopping centre, next to a long, steep road full of takeaways and restaurants: Greek, Turkish, Indian, Chinese and a Japanese sushi bar. Several men are sitting outside a café under tarpaulin smoking shisha.

She walks under an archway next to a black gate and find herself in a small courtyard. The houses are more modern than those in the adjourning square but painted cream to match. They lack the period features: the black railings, the chequered tiles, the basements. The houses in the courtyard all have narrow balconies on the first floor and wide garage doors next to the front ones. Nell locates the correct number but waits until exactly six before knocking. She can see the kitchen through the foggy downstairs window. Glasses, mugs, plates and a large saucepan rest haphazardly on a draining board. *Two girls. Three-bedroom house. Close to town centre.* It isn't much to go on.

A young woman, not much older than Nell, with long brown hair, dressed all in black and with a lot of eye make-up comes rushing through the gate and into the courtyard.

'Kelly-Ann?'

'Hi, yeah. Are you here about the room? Is it Nell?'

'Yes.'

'You know we don't want a student. We said it on the ad.'

'I'm not a student.'

Kelly-Ann looks at Nell in confusion. 'Oh. You look young, that's all. Sorry. Come on in then.'

Kelly-Ann takes a bunch of keys on a Hello Kitty key ring from her handbag and opens the door. Her nails are painted a vivid pink. Nell smells what she thinks must be Kelly-Ann's shampoo, something fruity and synthetic. She realises she has no idea how this will work. Will the other girl be there? Will they interview her? Will they ask her if she knows how to cook? She hopes they don't. She can boil an egg and make pasta but Alice did all the cooking. She mustn't tell them she doesn't have a job yet.

'Sorry I was late. I had a client whose colour took ages. I had to keep going out the back to mix more. She told us on the phone her hair was shoulder length. It was practically at her ribs.'

'It's okay. I was enjoying wandering around. Exploring.'

'We're right next to Preston Street. Three minutes from Churchill Square. God, listen to me, I sound like a fucking estate agent.'

They step into the dim, narrow hallway. The carpet is a faded dusty pink. A naked light bulb hangs from the ceiling. Kelly-Ann darts into the kitchen. 'It's pretty crappy but it's got everything, really. No dishwasher though. We're going to ask the landlord for a new cooker.'

Nell looks at the orange crusty circles around the electric hob rings.

'You can have a shelf in the fridge, of course.' Kelly-Ann gestures towards the magnet-covered fridge. 'And a cupboard. We tend to use our own stuff but there's salt and pepper and oils over by the cooker. We all use those. Most of the kitchen stuff is communal: saucepans, plates and things. Oh, except the Spot the Dog bowl. That's Robyn's. She freaks out if anyone uses it.'

Nell nods slowly, takes a hesitant step forward. The kitchen smells of burnt cheese.

'We put all the bills here.' Kelly-Ann gestures to the pin board above the small kitchen table. 'We split them three ways, despite the size of the rooms. The landlord receives one rent payment from Robyn for all of us, and we give Robyn our share of the bills. It works.'

Kelly-Ann appears to believe that Nell is the sort of person who could rent a room in this house, use communal cooking oils and pay bills that are split three ways. This is encouraging. There is a part of Nell that can easily imagine getting the train home tomorrow, or next week. She'll walk through the door with her rucksack. Alice will say nothing, only ask her what she wants for dinner. Nell will take her shoes off and put them in the hallway with Alice's and it will be as if nothing ever happened, as if she never left.

'It's the smallest room but you'll pay less for it,' Kelly-Ann is explaining. 'Come on. I'll show you.'

Nell follows Kelly-Ann up the stairs. The living area has two sagging sofas covered in worn throws, a wooden giraffe and a drying rack full of clothes and underwear. Outside, there is a small balcony with a metal table and one chair. Nell can see an ash tray balancing on the balcony rail. Kelly-Ann explains that they don't use the living area much and that Nell's room is next door, on the middle floor, but that her room, Robyn's room, and the bathroom, are all on the top floor.

'Is the giraffe yours?'

Kelly-Ann laughs. 'No. It isn't Robyn's either. I don't know where it came from. It was here when she moved in. So what do you do, Nell?'

'I work in retail.'

This is the most likely job she'll get, given her only experience, work-wise, is selling crisps and petrol.

'Well, like I said, or did I say? I'm a hairdresser. And Robyn does something admin-related at the university. Did you grow up in Brighton?'

'No. I came a couple of times as a child.'

'Oh, you'll love it,' Kelly-Ann tells her confidently. 'They say you have to be one of three things in this city. A vegetarian, a lesbian or the owner of a bicycle.'

'I don't think I'm any of those things.'

Kelly-Ann laughs. 'I have another theory. I think some people are pebbles.'

She glances at Nell's rucksack. 'People who just kind of wash up here. You know?'

Nell smiles. She likes Kelly-Ann with her pink nails, shiny hair, perfectly made-up eyes and pebble theories.

'I'd better show you the room, hadn't I? Harriet bought a storage heater from Argos but I think she took it with her. She left the bed and mattress though. She's moving in with her boyfriend so she doesn't need them. He's a dentist. Quite well off. Saves you, or whoever, having to find a bed I guess.'

17

The room is small: a pine chest of drawers with a knob missing, a hanging rail instead of a wardrobe and a single bed pushed against the wall. Someone has made a make-shift curtain from a rod and a square of red fabric. An abstract print in a small black frame hangs on the wall over the bed.

'It's great.'

'Well, I wouldn't go that far. You could take that down of course.' Kelly-Ann gestures to the print. 'Someone left it here. I've got no idea what it is. I prefer pictures of places, you know, London, New York, Paris. I've always wanted to go to Paris. I went to Brittany once on a school trip. I was sick on the ferry.'

'It's Rothko.'

'I wouldn't know. I was terrible at art at school. I never learned the names of the artists and the teacher was always going on at me to colour in one direction.'

'But you do a creative job now?'

Kelly-Ann puts a hand to her cheek. 'Oh, I don't know about that. I'd like to move to London next year, get a job in a proper swanky salon. I need a bit more experience first though. And anyway, I like it here. I grew up in Berkshire which was boring as hell.'

'I'd like to take the room,' Nell says, turning to Kelly-Ann. 'If you'll have me.'

Kelly-Ann shrugs as if it makes no difference to her but Nell can see she's happy.

'Well, that's fine by me. But I'd better call Robyn. Can you wait here a sec?'

'Sure.'

Kelly-Ann disappears downstairs to make the phone call, leaving Nell alone in the room. She sits on the edge of the bed feeling grateful to Harriet, whoever she is, for leaving it behind. Could she really live here? Why not? She needs a room and this is a room. Why look any further? And she would prefer to live with just girls for now.

A few minutes later, Kelly-Ann reappears in the doorway. 'Robyn says it's fine. She trusts my judgement.'

Nell stands. 'Thank you.'

'Well, Harriet's gone already. So I guess you can move your stuff in anytime.'

'I've only got this,' Nell says, gesturing to her rucksack.

Kelly-Ann raises an eyebrow. 'That's not much.'

'I need to go shopping,' she says hastily.

Kelly-Ann looks around the room. 'Well, let me know if you need a hand. I can help you carry stuff back from town. You'll need bed linen. Maybe a lamp or something?'

'Do you think it would be okay if I stayed here tonight? I had to leave my other place. You see—'

Kelly-Ann waves Nell's explanations away. 'I had a feeling you might ask that. I had to get away quickly once too. I was living in this place and the landlady went crazy. She put labels on everything in the fridge, and wrote on the walls. I'll leave you Robyn's details so you can pay her the deposit. I'm going to run a bath whilst she's out. I've got bubbles someone bought me ages ago. Haven't had a chance to use them. Robyn hogs the bathroom.'

'I'll go to the bank tomorrow.'

Kelly-Ann waves her hand dismissively and steps onto the landing. 'That will be fine. Oh, there's spare bedding in the cupboard under the stairs but I don't know whose it was or what it's like.'

'It'll be okay for tonight,' Nell says. 'Thank you.'

When Kelly-Ann finally closes the door, Nell allows herself to lean fully back on the bare mattress whilst being careful to keep her feet off the end. She closes her eyes. She can hear people crossing the courtyard. Someone is playing Spanish music from one of the balconies. Kelly-Ann is moving around in the kitchen whilst her bath fills. When Nell opens her eyes, she sits up, pulls the red curtain back and looks at the view of the courtyard from her window. There's the cry of a seagull and, although she can't see the sea, she is aware of how close it is. Its presence comforts her. She looks around the room, at the empty hanging rail, the broken chest of drawers and the Rothko on the wall. The room already feels like hers.

3

1993

Nell sits in the bath at Grandma's house. Alice is shampooing Nell's scalp, sculpting her hair upwards into a sharp point. She hands Nell the mirror and Nell frowns at her pointy hat. She looks like a Christmas elf. She isn't fond of elves. They have a tendency to complain, go awry. You never know where you are with an elf. She reaches up and flattens Alice's carefully sculpted point.

'Oh, well,' Alice says.

Nell enjoys having her hair washed in Grandma's blue bathroom with its tiles of sea horses, shells and sailing boats. She likes the plant on the windowsill with its soft green leaves, and the painting on the wall of Alice when she was younger. Nell is learning to read and she studies the words and letters written underneath the painting. *Self portrait of a young girl.*

Grandma's house is far away from London and it took Nell and Alice a long time to get here. They boarded their train at King's Cross and Nell did her colouring at the table even though it was hard to stay within the lines.

When they arrived in Lincolnshire, Grandma came to meet them at the tiny station. She'd stood, as she always does, on the other side of the platform, waving. Nell ran over the bridge, taking the steps two at a time, her rucksack bouncing on her back. Grandma hugged her, and Nell had breathed in her Grandma smell: dried flowers, lavender soap and baking, but also something else – something just Grandma. They'd put their bags in the boot of her purple car. Nell had stared out of the window at the cows and the fields and the giant skies.

Downstairs, Nell can hear Grandma in the kitchen doing Grandma type things: drying the dishes, humming a tune, putting the cutlery away.

Alice squeezes water over Nell's shoulders using Grandma's yellow sponge as Nell thinks about the baby bird. She'd found it in the garden earlier that afternoon and had watched it carefully, not wanting to scare it. The bird was all fluffed up, its eyes darting around. 'It's okay,' Nell had whispered. The bird didn't move and she'd noticed one of its wings sticking out at a strange angle. It had made a horrible noise, like a scream. She'd gone to fetch Grandma.

'We can't leave it here,' Nell had said. Grandma agreed. There were often cats or foxes in the garden, and so Grandma had gone back to the house and returned with a shoe box lined with a tea towel. She watched as Grandma scooped the bird gently into her hands and placed it in the box where it had sat there quietly, making no effort to explore its new home. They sprinkled seed in the corner because Nell had been worried the bird would grow hungry, then put the box on the hearth rug and lit a fire to keep it warm. Nell had checked the bird every ten minutes until Alice told her they had to go out to the local hardware store for turpentine.

When they returned, Grandma cooked dinner whilst Nell sat, writing the words Alice had given her to learn that weekend into her spelling book: *frill, frog, from, frost, grab, grill, grin, grip*. After they'd finished eating, Nell asked to get down and had gone straight over to the fireplace. She returned carrying the shoe box.

'He died,' she told Grandma.

Alice peered into the box and sighed.

'Poor little thing,' Grandma had said, touching Nell's shoulder.

And so Grandma helped her dig a hole in the garden by the ash tree. They'd covered the bird with earth and laid a single daffodil over the grave. Alice gave Nell a piece of string so she could make a cross from two twigs.

Nell thinks about this, the events of the day, as Alice fills a jug with warm water from the sink, ready to wash the conditioner from Nell's hair. She closes her eyes as Alice gently tilts her head back and begins to rinse.

'Why did the bird die?' Nell asks, her eyelashes wet, the warm water trickling over her shoulders and back.

Alice places the jug on the windowsill. She squeezes the excess water from Nell's hair, teasing out a knot with her fingers. Nell's hair is thick and curly and prone to knots unlike Alice's which is sleek and sharply cut – a little like Alice herself.

'The bird was very badly injured,' Alice says. 'Perhaps he flew too early.' She pauses, lets go of Nell's hair. 'Sometimes sad things just happen.'

Nell stretches her foot and hooks the plug chain with her toe. Alice's answer is unsatisfactory. She doesn't like to believe that things *just happen*. There must, she feels, be a reason for all the giving and taking away of things.

'Be careful,' Alice warns her. 'You'll pull the plug. I might use the water.'

Nell lets her foot drop back under the milky foam. 'Everything dies,' she tells Alice.

Alice says nothing. Instead, she reaches for the blue towel and stands in front of the bathtub holding it wide. Alice will wrap Nell tightly then take the smaller pink towel, twist Nell's hair up inside it, working her magic, until the turban of towel sits on her head and she feels like an Egyptian queen. Alice has taught her all about the Egyptians; the beautiful, powerful queens – Cleopatra and Nefertiti, the pyramids, the tombs and the sacred cats. Alice borrowed a book from the library and read to her about how the Egyptians were buried with their possessions, all the things they would need to take with them into the next life. The fact that it is possible to take things with you to the next life is reassuring.

Now that she has finished her bath she'll go downstairs where Grandma will be writing a letter, or knitting, or listening to a play on the radio.

'All clean?' Grandma will ask.

Nell sits on the window ledge of the flat. Only the top section of the window is open because they are six storeys up. She twists a strand of hair tightly around her finger until its tip turns pink. People are rushing about on the street below. It has been raining on and off all day, a brief, irritating London rain that causes the regular opening and closing of umbrellas. The pavements glisten like smooth, grey flint.

Nell can just about squeeze onto the sill of the square window. Soon she will be too big but that doesn't matter because soon she won't be here anymore. She rests her diary on her knees. It's a purple-lined notepad that one of Alice's friends gave her. Nell has decorated it with stickers from Woolworths: Care Bears and My Little Ponies, and written *Nell's Secret Diary* on the front. She likes the idea of a secret diary, although she doesn't have many secrets.

She keeps her diary under her pillow along with her book about California and her hag stone. She found the stone last summer. It's smooth and pale and has a hole in the middle. That day on the beach, she had held the stone up to her eye and looked through it. She could see the pier, the helter skelter, the neon sign – *Brighton*, and two flags flapping in the breeze.

'What have you found?' Alice asked.

Nell had shown Alice the stone.

'Ah. A hag stone.'

'What's a hag stone?'

'A stone with a hole in the middle. They're supposed to be lucky. They're supposed to protect you.'

Nell had kept the stone, putting it in the pocket of her shorts and bringing it home on the train.

Several months ago a friend of Alice's, a sculptor called Mike who wears lot of denim and a brown moustache that looks like a fat, lazy caterpillar, gave Nell the book about California – a battered, second-hand travel guide. Nell copies the photographs from the book into her sketch pad. She paints a row of houses at night. The houses are all different colours, like sweets, and the evening sky is a vivid blue. Perhaps it is brighter in America with its rainbow houses and orange bridges. Perhaps it exists more fully; louder, sharper and with more pazaz, a word Nell likes, that seems to perfectly suit the photographs. She keeps the book under her pillow at night hoping she will dream of huge red trees, golden beaches and roller skates.

Nell has asked why she doesn't have a daddy like the children in the park, at the art gallery, or in the books she reads. Alice has explained that not all children have mummies and daddies, that some live with grandparents or aunties and uncles, or other people who take care of them. This answer satisfied Nell for a while, until it didn't.

'Where is my daddy?' she asked Alice. They were sitting together in the doctor's waiting room. Nell can't remember why she had chosen that particular moment to ask Alice but she knows that once she had, it became an urgent question that must immediately be answered.

'He's far away,' Alice had said.

The woman in the chair opposite lifted her eyes from her magazine.

'Where far away?'

Alice glanced at the woman then pointed to the large map on the wall. Nell likes looking at the map each time they visit the doctors. The map is brown and blue and says *Map of The World* in the top left-hand corner.

'There,' Alice said.

She had looked at where Alice's finger was pointing: United States of America.

'Will he come back?'

'No,' Alice said. 'It's just the two of us, but that's okay isn't it?'

Nell had nodded, sensing that a different answer would upset Alice. Anyway, it isn't always just the two of them. Alice has friends, like Mike, who has given her the book about California as a clue to where her daddy is.

Nell sleeps in the living area behind a large folding

screen because the flat has one bedroom. She is often aware of Alice's friends tiptoeing past her makeshift room. They sit around drinking beer, talking quietly and using a lot of words Nell likes the sound of but doesn't understand: Kon-sep-choo-al, Sy-ker-del-ik, Fow-viz-um.

Today, the living area of the flat is covered in boxes and bubble-wrapped canvases. Someone came yesterday and took the sofa away.

Tomorrow I am moving house, Nell writes in her diary. *I will not live in London anymore. I will live in Lincolnshire with Alice in Grandma's house.* She writes *Lincolnshire* slowly, making sure of the correct spelling. She doesn't like having to cross words out if she can help it. She looks again at the street below, at the black taxis and red buses, at the people making their way home from work in their black and grey clothes. She rests her pen against her cheek then adds a final line. *But Grandma will not be there.*

Nell is standing, wearing her best dress, holding the words to a song she doesn't know. Alice has found a ribbon for her hair in Grandma's sewing tin. She looks at the wooden box that she knows is supposed to contain Grandma.

Many people have come to say goodbye to Grandma. Mostly Grandma's friends who all look like slightly different versions of Grandma with their pleated skirts, soft cardigans, beige tights and tightly fixed hair. Wherever Nell looks she sees Grandmas, but not *her* Grandma.

'Your Grandma had a lot of friends,' a man with a white tufty beard says.

Alice told Nell at breakfast last week what had happened. Grandma's friend, Moira, had worried when Grandma hadn't turned up to the knitting club on Friday and when she wasn't in church on Sunday.

'Grandma had an accident on the stairs. Grandma has died.'

Nell had pushed the soggy cereal around her bowl with her spoon, unsure of what she was supposed to say. Alice's eyes were red and sore.

'I told her not to wear those stupid slippers,' Alice had said.

After they have sung the last hymn, a red curtain begins to move on its own. It circles slowly around Grandma. Won't someone make it stop? For a few seconds time is broken up, shattered. This is not the way she wants to remember Grandma. There is a hole in the wall and the coffin begins to slide inside. She is being touched on the shoulder by a relative she barely knows, urged to walk forward, out into the grounds of the crematorium where some of the others are already waiting.

Later, Nell is in Grandma's garden. She is supposed to be playing outside with her second cousins, two round-faced boys with bruises on their knees, who stare at her clothes and ask her too many questions.

'I don't go to school because Alice teaches me things at home.'

'That's illegal,' the older boy says. 'Children have to go to school. Your mum could go to prison for not sending you to school.'

The younger boy nods solemnly.

Nell shrugs but she is secretly worried. She decides to go inside and find Alice. She looks for her mother's long blue skirt. She wishes she were younger. She wishes she could hide behind the fabric of the skirt and suck her thumb and not have to answer any questions from boys. She wishes she hadn't known it was Grandma inside the box and that she would never see her again. Being seven is hard. She feels anxious and scratches at her arm, catching a small scab that had almost healed. She pulls the sleeve of her cardigan down so no one will notice. Grandma used to look at Nell's skin and frown with concern. *Your nerves are at the ends of your fingertips. Just like your mother's.*

Once Alice has finished talking, Nell turns to her and asks, 'Will you go to prison for not sending me to school?'

Alice looks at her calmly. 'No,' she says, before taking a sip of wine. 'That isn't something you need to worry about.'

When they return home to London, Nell senses that there is a decision to be made. Mike is there one evening.

The fresh air will be better for her skin. You won't get anything for it if you sell it. It needs work.

I paint people not fields.

Get off this estate for fuck's sake, Alice. I found a needle in the hallway yesterday. The lifts stink of piss. If you don't want to go because you want to be close to the scene—

What fucking scene? No one cares about portraits anymore. There's only a scene if you've got a shark in a box. Perhaps I should crush all my work under a steamroller or shove a chicken in my knickers.

So go. The city makes you anxious anyway. You hardly leave the flat.

I need to paint people, Mike. You don't know what it's like to come from a tiny place where everyone knows everyone and everyone is the same.

Alice tells Nell that the following week they will be moving to Grandma's cottage. Nell will have her own bedroom – Alice's old room. Alice will have Grandma's room. Nell has always liked Grandma's cottage, the sound of the cockerel in the morning, the mooing of cows, the small planes making their way to the nearby RAF base. Still, she can't imagine leaving the pigeons, the tall buildings, and the dark London skies she watches from the window in the evenings whilst Alice paints her. She'll no longer hear the rattle of the trains when she's trying to sleep, the sirens from the street below, or the sound of the neighbours arguing. She isn't sure she wants to leave the

31

park with the ducks, the local library, the red buses she travels on and the galleries Alice takes her to visit.

The worst thing of all is that they are moving to Grandma's cottage but Grandma will not be there. Grandma slid into the wall and her ashes were given to Alice in a small vase that is now in Alice's sock drawer. Nell saw it there when she went to borrow a pair of socks after Alice forgot to wash hers.

4

2002

The following day, whilst buying bed linen from Sainsbury's, she receives a text from Alice: *Where are you and where are you staying?*

I've found a room in a house near the town centre. There are two girls. They are really nice, she adds, which, she feels, is true.

Robyn is tall with short, dark, bobbed hair. Last night she had been wearing a white shirt, black pencil skirt and bright red lipstick. She was putting bleach and washing up liquid in the cupboard under the sink when Nell had appeared in the kitchen doorway.

'Jesus. You're young.'

'I'm not a student.'

'So Kelly-Ann tells me.' Robyn had wiped her hands on her skirt then extended her hand. 'Welcome to the house, Nell. I'm afraid we pretty much keep ourselves to ourselves. There are no film or fondue nights here.'

'That's fine by me,' Nell had said, shaking Robyn's

hand, even though she had no idea what a fondue night was.

'Let me know if you need anything.' Robyn shoved the plastic carrier bag into an over-stuffed drawer. 'You can call me anytime, or give me a knock.'

Although Robyn's tone was brisk, Nell had felt a warmth, a kindness, beneath her chilly exterior.

After she sends the text to Alice, she puts the phone back in her pocket and pushes her trolley into the next aisle. She buys a sheet, a duvet and duvet cover, pillows and a large blue towel. *I now own a towel.* She leaves the shop with two bulky bags. The day is bright, promising. Perhaps she should walk along the pier. No, she has more important things to do.

She had left the house early in the morning, not wanting Robyn and Kelly-Ann to know she wasn't working. Finding a place to live so quickly had felt like an incredible piece of good luck and she wanted that luck to continue. *Today, I will find a job.*

By the end of her first week in Brighton, Nell has an interview at a clothes shop in the shopping centre. She confirms all that the store manager, Teresa, wants to hear: weekends aren't a problem, neither is time-keeping or personal grooming. She talks about her job at the garage, how she was responsible for the till and the cashing up at the end of her shift, then answers Teresa's questions regarding how she might handle a situation with a 'difficult' customer who wants to return a blouse she's clearly worn. Teresa asks Nell what additional items she might sell to a woman who is looking to buy a dress for her grandson's christening. Nell suggests jewellery, shoes, a handbag and Teresa is pleased. This is what's known as an 'upsell' she tells Nell whilst making a note on the interview questionnaire she had been printing as Nell arrived.

Nell confirms she is able to lift totes, climb ladders, change window displays, and that she doesn't mind cleaning the staff toilet when it's her turn on the rota to do so. Teresa calls the next day, offers Nell the job and asks if she can start on Monday. She'll be paid at the end of the month which means she can give Robyn her rent on time.

Nell spends her days hanging garments, tidying fitting rooms, zipping women into dresses that are one size too small for them, carrying boxes of shoes, offering pop socks and sliding cheap clothes into plastic bags whilst reciting the twenty-eight-day refund policy. At lunchtime she eats a supermarket sandwich whilst sitting on a crate in the stockroom or, if it's sunny and dry, perched on the steps at Churchill Square amongst the pigeons, keeping an eye out for thieving seagulls.

In the house, she makes herself inexpensive meals that require little preparation: pasta with pre-cooked prawns,

35

vermicelli noodles with pre-chopped vegetables, packet stir-fries or, when she can't be bothered with anything else, microwave porridge. Her legs ache at the end of each day. The skin on her heels hardens and she continues to hear the beep of the till when she goes to bed. She takes all the worst shifts and never refuses overtime. She never asks for two days off together because this keeps her from having time to go anywhere. She occasionally has the feeling she is punishing herself although for what, she isn't sure.

On her days off she hoovers the house, cleans the bathroom, does her washing then walks to the local supermarket to buy food. In the evenings she reads, lying on her bed, sometimes drinking beer which she has discovered is easy enough to buy in the supermarket if she wears make-up and keeps her work badge on. When she has drunk too much and the words begin to blur she stares at the Artex ceiling wondering vaguely if it contains asbestos.

Gradually, over the coming weeks, Nell acquires new clothes and a few things for her room using the rest of her savings: a dressing gown, a lamp, a washing basket. She learns about her housemates. Kelly-Ann enjoys listening to nineties dance music before work. She sings in the shower, stays out late at the weekends and uses a lot of bleach if she cleans the kitchen. Over the coming weeks,

Kelly-Ann offers Nell free hair treatments in exchange for shared bottles of Prosecco because Kelly-Ann only drinks wine with bubbles.

Kelly-Ann is twenty but Robyn is twenty-seven. To Nell and Kelly-Ann, Robyn is an age apart from them, closer to thirty than twenty, a grown up.

Robyn wears a lot of black, and tight-fitting pencil skirts. She dries her sixty denier tights on the storage heater in the living room in the evenings. She buys a new pair of tights the minute one pair becomes bobbly. Nell knows this as she sees the cardboard packaging in the recycling. As far as Nell can make out, Robyn likes red wine, smoking Silk Cuts on the balcony, and reading Barbara Vine novels. She appears to eat a lot of low-fat yoghurt, and there are always towers of tinned tuna in Robyn's cupboard, as if she has a fear tinned tuna will run out. Robyn paints her nails black: fingers and toes. Little bottles of black nail varnish can be found around the house, on the bathroom windowsill, on top of the microwave, behind a cushion on the sofa.

Robyn's room is the largest, but also the messiest. Nell is always surprised whenever she catches a glimpse of it or is forced to search for something that has gone missing from the kitchen. Clothes, wilted and abandoned, lie draped over Robyn's choking furniture. The floor is similarly covered in dark garments, magazines, and empty low-fat yoghurt pots. The thick, green velvet curtains are always drawn. Robyn's bedside table is full of glasses and mugs that Nell sometimes has to retrieve if she wants a cup of tea. At least three evenings a week Robyn will take a long bath. When Nell hears the water running she knows she won't be able to use the bathroom for an hour. Robyn's bedroom is the closest to the bathroom. She plays Italian opera, leaving the door open so she can hear the music from the bath.

'Bloody hell,' Kelly-Ann mutters when Nell enters the kitchen. 'I wish she wouldn't play that so loudly. I feel like I'm in a spaghetti sauce advert. And I wish she'd close the door. I have to run across to my room with my eyes closed.'

Robyn takes a bottle of red wine into the bathroom, along with a packet of lychees. She forgets to clear up, leaving lychee peel and shiny brown stones littering the rim of the bath, and circular red wine glass stains next to the taps. Nell imagines Robyn sitting in her nest of bubbles, drinking her wine, eating her Chinese fruit and listening to her Italian opera, one black-toed foot perched on the edge of the tub. She pictures Robyn wrapping herself in her large fluffy towel before heading back to her dingy, dishevelled cave.

When Robyn talks to her it is of practical, house-related things. Robyn is the only one of the three of them who has met the landlord: *That fat bastard who thinks it's okay to have a cooker with only three working hob rings.*

She wonders why this bothers Robyn seeing as she rarely cooks.

Every other weekend, Robyn goes to London to stay with her girlfriend, Freja, which means Nell and Kelly-Ann have the house, and the bathroom, to themselves. Kelly-Ann plays her dance music whenever she likes and they are both slightly less diligent about doing the washing-up. On the weekends when Robyn is around, Freja stays at the house and cooks, or else they go out to the pub with Robyn's friends. On these weekends, Kelly-Ann visits her sister in Tunbridge Wells. When Nell asks Kelly-Ann why she does this, Kelly-Ann grimaces and says, 'Your bedroom isn't next to theirs.'

Robyn will always clean the house and wash the bed sheets before Freja arrives. She'll buy blueberries because Freja likes blueberries. Nell has watched them in the kitchen together. She has seen Robyn put her hand on Freja's back when Freja is cooking, the way Freja will touch Robyn's hips as she manoeuvres around her to get to the fridge. She sees the physical need Robyn and Freja have to be close to one another.

Nell occasionally notices men looking at her in the supermarket, on her walk to work, or on those evenings when Kelly-Ann, or her colleagues at the shop, persuade her to come out for a drink. When Nell notices a man looking at her, when she spots that familiar look of interest, of want, she moves away as quickly as possible. She avoids taking the bus. Inevitably, Nell will pick the window seat and a man will choose to sit next to her, blocking her exit, making her feel panicky, and overwhelming her with his closeness, his *maleness*.

'Why don't you date, Nell?' Kelly-Ann has asked her. 'You're so pretty and sweet. Guys are always looking at you.'

The girls at work are also always enquiring as to whether she's seeing anyone. 'You'll never meet anyone working here,' Teresa said to her when they were checking off a tote box of handbags. 'The only men that come in here are with their wives. Either that, or they're buying something for their wives. You need to get out more, Nell. You should try internet dating. Lots of people are doing it now.'

Nell had bought a laptop with her second month's salary. She enjoys browsing the internet, dreaming about clothes she can't afford, reading the news and latest book reviews.

She sits on her bed one evening, opens her laptop and looks at the dating websites Teresa has mentioned. She can't bring herself to join any of them. She has no idea what to say about herself and doesn't like the thought of putting a photograph on a website. She sees other girls, in the shops, in the town centre, in the pubs, with their boyfriends and feels, like with the girls at school, that they are a different species.

5

2003

It's a Friday evening in May and Nell is locking up the shop with Teresa. They cash up, turn the tills off, set the alarm and exit the artificially lit world of the shopping centre into the warm May evening. Nell has enjoyed the change in seasons, the feel of the sun on her arms on her lunch break and not having to lean out of the bed to switch the storage heater on twenty minutes before she is able get up. She arrived in Brighton in late October and the winter had felt long and bleak. In January, the beach had been covered in snow and she'd walked to work in her wellies. She likes to take a walk along the seafront every day, either before or after work, whatever the weather, even though the shop is only five minutes from the house. There have been days when she has hardly been able to see the sea for mist and spray, days when an umbrella would have been useless. Then there have been evenings when the sun has split the sky over the line of the horizon and the wind has breathed through the rigging of the dinghies on Hove beach and she's been able to remind herself how much she loves living here.

Once the alarm is set, Nell and Teresa part, Teresa reminding Nell that she isn't in tomorrow and that Nell needs to send the weekly figures to the regional manager before five. She asks her if she can please let Shirley, one of the part-timers, know that her holiday request has been accepted, reminds Nell to leave a handover for the assistant manager, Stacey, who is in on Sunday, and tells her to eat the hummus in the fridge if she wants because it will be no good by Monday.

Nell walks slowly home along the front. The beach is full of students and couples waiting to watch the sunset. She can hear music from a sound system someone has brought down to the pebbles. The waves roll gently in as the starlings settle on the carcass of the West Pier. Her phone buzzes in her pocket. It's Kelly-Ann telling her she's in the pub with her colleague, Sophie, who rents the beauty room. She asks if Nell wants to join them and Nell says she will, that she's on her way.

The pub has a gothic feel: wall lights with bare candle bulbs, dusty chandeliers, a red and black colour scheme. There's a strange devil head over the bar that looks as though it has been made with papier-mâché. The pub is permanently ready for Halloween. People spill out of the doors and onto the narrow pavement outside.

Nell finds Sophie and Kelly-Ann standing near the

back. Neither of them want a drink as Sophie has just bought a round, and so Nell edges her way to the bar. She'll order an apple juice. She isn't eighteen for another five months and feels embarrassed when asked for I.D. She stands, trying to catch the attention of the busy barmaid for what seems like ages, before someone taps her on the shoulder.

'You need to be taller, that's the problem.'

A man in a red baseball cap is smiling at her. He has dimples at the corners of his mouth and a small white scar above his right eyebrow.

'What can I get you?' The barmaid shouts across to the man.

'Go on,' he says. 'Now's your chance. What would you like? I'm having the Camden Ale.'

'That sounds good,' she says, forgetting about apple juice.

The man in the red baseball cap orders for the both of them. Before she can refuse, he produces a twenty pound note from the top pocket of his shirt and gives it to the barmaid.

'Don't you worry, there's plenty more where that came from. I've had extra commission this month.'

Nell smiles politely.

'I work in sales,' the man says, as if she was wondering. 'I'm Scott.'

'Nell.'

'That's pretty. Kind of old-fashioned. You suit it.'

'It's short for Eleonora.'

'Even nicer.'

Scott hands her the drink and she takes a sip. She wishes she had insisted on paying for her own drink as she now feels an obligation to talk him. They are standing under a speaker. The bar is playing some kind of nineties grunge music. Pearl Jam? Alice in Chains? She isn't sure.

'Don't tell me you're on your own,' Scott says, over the music.

'I'm with friends.' Nell gestures in the direction of Kelly-Ann and Sophie but when she turns to look for them, they aren't there. 'Well, they're around somewhere.'

Scott smiles. 'I'm going outside for a cigarette. Fancy some air?'

Perhaps Kelly-Ann and Sophie went outside. She doesn't know how people can stand to be in such busy and crowded places for so long. One visit to a nightclub had been enough. It had made her feel ill, the thumping music, the bright, piercing strobe lights illuminating half-naked, sweaty bodies. She'd gone out after work for a pizza on a Saturday evening with Tilly and Sabina, both students who only worked at the shop over the Christmas period. 'Oh, come on Nell, I can't believe you've never been to a nightclub. I know the doorman. He won't ask you for I.D.' The loud music had burrowed into her skull and she'd felt dizzy. Disorientated, it had taken her ten minutes to find the cloakroom. Once she had retrieved her coat, she'd stood outside, leaning against the wall, trying to breathe and wondering why she seemed unable to cope with so much of life that other people appeared to find easy, enjoy even. She had remembered Grandma's words: *Your nerves are at the end of your fingertips, just like your mother's.*

'What happened to you last night?' Tilly had asked her at work the following day.

'I had to get back,' she'd lied. My housemate locked herself out.'

Nell stands on the pavement outside the pub. The evening remains warm and dry although it has grown cooler. There are several tables outside the pub. On the other side of the road is the park. The evening light plays through the branches of the trees that line the path. She can hear the roll of skate-boards, the crying of a small child. Scott sits at one of the tables. Nell can't see Sophie or Kelly-Ann anywhere.

'You'd better grab that spot,' he says, gesturing to the space opposite him, 'before someone else does.'

Nell perches uneasily at the end of the table. She keeps her jacket on. Now that she has sat down, she feels tired. Her feet hurt. The others had told her, when she'd started the job, that she'd get used to being on her feet all day, that they would hurt less. They don't. She still has to soak them in the evenings and then, once they are soft enough, scrub at her heels with the pumice stone. She isn't allowed to wear trainers for work because it doesn't 'fit with the brand'. Sitting down doesn't fit with the brand either. Whatever shoes she wears, it makes no difference. She lies at the end of her bed in the evenings with her feet up against the wall, under the Rothko print, trying to get the feeling back.

Scott offers Nell a cigarette.

'No thanks.'

'Don't smoke?'

'Not anymore.'

'You gave up?'

'I was never a serious smoker. I smoked as a teenager.'

Scott studies Nell carefully. 'You don't look much older than that now.'

She can feel a flush spreading across her cheeks. She lets her hair fall over her face. 'I'm seventeen.'

Scott looks pleased with himself. He lights his cigarette. 'So I was right then. You know, people are always telling me to give up. They say I haven't got enough willpower to stop. The way I see it, I've got more willpower than any of them because they keep telling me to stop but I don't, I stand firm.' Scott chuckles.

Nell smiles weakly. She hasn't eaten since lunchtime. The bar must sell crisps but it feels like a lot of effort for her feet. She takes a gulp of her beer, wondering how quickly she can get through it. She's looking forward, now, to returning to her room. Perhaps she'll stop on the way home and buy supermarket sushi. She doesn't feel like washing up.

Scott takes a drag on his cigarette, being careful to blow his smoke sideways away from her. He rubs the stubble on his chin then taps the end of his cigarette into the ashtray on the table.

'I bet you're a student, right?'

'No. I work in a shop.'

'That's good,' Scott says thoughtfully. 'I always meet students, especially in this pub. They know nothing about anything. They've never worked a day in their lives. Know what I mean?'

Nell bites her lip, frowns. 'I guess so...'

'You don't know anything about life until you get out to work,' Scott continues. 'You work hard. I could tell that as soon as I saw you.'

'It's just a job in a shop.'

'I bet you'll get promoted though. You'll be running the place before too long.'

Nell tries to smile but the idea sends a cold shiver through her. She had thought, recently, about applying for a supervisor position. The hourly rate would be an additional one pound fifty on top of what she's getting now. The extra money each month would be useful. Somehow, though, she couldn't bring herself to apply.

She glances in the direction of the pub door. She could really do with that packet of crisps.

Scott follows the direction of her gaze. 'I don't like this pub much.'

'It's okay. Just busy.'

'I know some really good pubs,' Scott tells her. 'They're not in town though. Proper pubs where you can sit by the fire and get a decent Sunday lunch, you know.'

'That sounds nice.'

'Do you drive?'

'No,' Nell says, thinking of the money she had told Alice she was saving for driving lessons, the money she had used to leave home.

'You need to drive to get to these pubs. There's one I really like, The Bird in Hand. The roasts are great. They do something to the carrots that makes them sweet.' He stubs his cigarette out.

'Carrots *are* sweet.'

'Sweeter then.' Scott grins.

'I haven't had a Sunday roast for ages.'

'We should go this Sunday.'

Nell gives Scott a tentative smile. She drains the last of her beer. Perhaps he's serious. Sunday will be another day of washing and ironing, of going to the supermarket, of pulling hair from the bathroom plughole and wiping make-up off the mirror.

'I do have Sunday off.'

'That's sorted then. I mean, why not? You're off. I'm off…'

Nell looks down into her empty glass. She tucks her hair behind her ear.

'It would be no trouble to drive you out, and I really do fancy a roast. You could be back by mid afternoon, if you've got something to do.'

She doesn't have anything to do, except her washing, but she doesn't tell Scott this. She's caught the bus to Devil's Dyke a few times but that's as much of the Sussex countryside as she's seen. Is it a date? So what if it is? Maybe she should be dating.

'I had better go and find my friends,' she says.

Nell gives Scott her number before she leaves, scribbling it down on the back of a Boots receipt she finds in her purse. Scott slips the receipt into the pocket of his trousers and Nell imagines it going through the wash.

Scott pats his pocket. 'Don't worry,' he says, as if reading her mind. 'Don't want to lose this. I'll see you on Sunday.'

6

1993

Mike helps load their things into his van. They have sold most of the furniture, or else left it behind.

The clearing out of the flat and loading of the van takes longer than expected and it is late afternoon by the time they set off.

Nell sits between Mike and Alice who keeps reaching across Nell to fiddle with the radio.

'Can't you stick to one thing?' Mike asks.

'No,' Alice says.

Mike pushes a cassette into the slot.

'Simon and Garfunkel?'

'I'm driving,' Mike replies. 'So I get to choose.'

They stop at a motorway service station and eat their egg and cress sandwiches in the car park. Nell and Alice go to find the toilets. Nell asks Alice if Mike is her boyfriend. It's a shame, she thinks, that Mike isn't coming to live with them.

Alice laughs. She says that Mike wouldn't live with a woman in that way and that Mike's life is in London.

Nell is disappointed. Two people do not make a family.

'Only another hour and a half,' Mike tells them cheerfully as they climb back into the van.

The roads become smaller and quieter. It's early evening, late spring. There's a low sun over the hedgerows and the fields are tall with wheat. The landscape is green and yellow, flat and far reaching. Telegraph poles stand like silent giants. A military plane flies low overhead as the landscape changes from flat to hilly.

'We're in the Wolds now,' Mike says.

Alice lights a cigarette and smokes it out the window. 'Yes, I know. I grew up here.'

'I was telling Nell.'

Nell watches her new world through the window. She feels excited when she recognises where they are. Grandma once told her that, when she was a girl, she cycled to school. Nell pictures Grandma with her hair in long plaits, riding her bike, her satchel on one shoulder. The image in her mind is in black and white because that's how she sees the past. She tries to add colour. At first, the scene is soft and watery but slowly the colours become bolder. There is the pale yellow sun, the cornflower-blue sky, the hedges full of ripening blackberries, and Grandma in a navy school uniform cycling along the edge of the tall wheat field.

They arrive at Grandma's cottage and Nell watches as

Mike and Alice carry boxes and canvases inside. 'I don't want my canvases out there all night,' Alice says.

Nell steps cautiously into the hallway. There is no Grandma to hug her, to ask her if they've had a good trip, or if she'd like a jam tart. She looks at the pictures on the mantelpiece, the embroidered duck cushions, the Renoir painting of the two girls at the piano. The house feels empty even though it is only Grandma who is missing.

When the van is cleared, Mike goes to the fish and chip shop. He returns with battered fish and chips, along with four bottles of beer, and a can of lemonade for Nell. 'I popped to the offie. Thought we'd earned it. I got haddock,' Mike says. 'There's more of that left, isn't there? I thought you'd prefer it.'

'Thank you,' Alice says, rummaging around in a box. She finds a bottle opener. 'You heard what happened at Grand Banks, didn't you? Cod is pretty much extinct there now.'

They have their haddock and chips at the kitchen table using Grandma's plates with the blue and pink flowers. Mike has made a small portion for Nell, mostly chips and a large dollop of ketchup from a glass bottle in Grandma's cupboard. Alice frowns at the ketchup but allows Nell to have it as it is a special occasion. Nell keeps expecting to see Grandma. She will appear from the garden or else she'll hear her coming down the stairs. She'll be wearing her yellow cardigan and her slippers. 'Shall we have tea?' she'll say.

It's quiet in Grandma's cottage. The London traffic, sirens, trains, noisy neighbours and the creaky lift doors have all gone forever.

Mike carries Nell's rucksack and her bag of clothes up the stairs to Alice's old bedroom. He surveys the room and smiles. 'It's a shrine to the seventies in here.'

Nell smiles back even though she doesn't know what a shrine is or what the seventies looked like.

She brushes her teeth in Grandma's bathroom. The water is different here, soft and bubbly. She returns to her new room and takes her pyjamas from her rucksack. The wallpaper is a faded print of brown and orange squares and is peeling in the corners. There is a wooden wardrobe and a matching bedside table. Nell studies the duvet with its busy scene of brown and turquoise butterflies in a meadow. She pushes the crocheted wool blanket to the end of her bed in case it makes her itch.

When she closes her eyes she is riding Grandma's bicycle. She cycles past the hedgerows and fields of tall wind-bent wheat. Her hair flies behind her in the breeze. She's wearing her favourite dress and white jelly sandals. She cycles all the way to the sea.

Alice finds Nell a bicycle. The bicycle was at the end of someone's driveway next to a pram with a sign saying

Please Take. Nell cycles along the quiet road. Alice allows her to play outside as long as she stays within view of the cottage. It is possible to go hours without seeing a car. Alice's concern are the dykes, the deep trenches of water at the side of the road that are used for drainage. 'Don't cycle close to the dykes,' Alice says. She tells Nell she knew a girl at school called Rosemary Cartwright who drowned after falling off her bicycle and into a dyke.

Neither must she walk across any fields alone in case they contain a bull who would charge and kill her. Bulls are attracted to red and Nell has a red jumper. She likes to think she would be able to take it off in time, toss it away from her to distract the bull who would be fooled by the flying, personless, jumper.

Alice and Nell's cottage is the smallest house on the long flat road. There are two or three houses, barns and outhouses dotted amongst the fields. Some of the houses have little bridges in front of them over the dykes. The fields eventually lead to the saltmarshes, the dunes, and the grey North Sea. In London, everything was tall but here it is flat, and with more sky. The people have all gone, replaced with rows of cabbages and sugar beet.

Alice pulls up the carpets. She tells Nell they will take the carpet to the dump but instead she leaves the thick roll in the garden leaning against the shed.

After she has discarded the carpets, Alice removes

Grandma's pictures and mirrors from the walls to make space for her canvases.

Nell chooses animal posters for her bedroom. The rest of the house has too many faces. She does not want any faces of people in her bedroom. Instead she has a grey seal, a kingfisher in flight, and a red squirrel. She chooses the posters from the local wildlife centre Alice takes her to. She keeps her book on California in her bedside drawer along with her hag stone.

When she isn't working, or stripping carpets, Alice is in the garden. She digs over the flowerbeds and plants herbs and vegetables, telling Nell they will eat straight from the garden. She covers their dinner plates in chives, parsley and thyme. Herbs from the garden have more minerals and they will both be healthier in the countryside. Alice hopes that Nell's skin will improve. Nell tries not to scratch but it's hard.

In the garden, Nell likes to spin. She raises her arms and whirls around until she feels light-headed and the lawn, trees and sky become a blur of blue, brown and green. She lies on the itchy grass feeling hot and dizzy.

'I wish you wouldn't do that,' Alice says. 'You might faint.'

'I won't faint.'

The lawn is sprinkled with daisies, buttercups and dandelions. Alice shows her how yellow turns to green in the shade by holding a buttercup under a plant pot. 'See?' she says.

Nell knows that yellow and blue make green. She knows all the colours that make other colours because Alice has shown her how to mix them on her palette. Cochineal red is made from the juice of thousands of tiny bugs that live on prickly pear cactus leaves. Bug Juice Red would be a better name.

Alice buys a camera. 'This is a very old camera,' she tells Nell. 'It's called a view camera. I spent some of our inheritance but don't worry, we'll make amazing photographs.'

Next Alice converts the cellar into a darkroom. 'I always thought this could be a darkroom. Your grandma never used it for anything. She thought it was spooky.'

Alice photographs Nell in the garden, in the fields behind the house and on the bridge that crosses the stream. Nell plays in the garden in her swimming costume, darting in and out of the spray from the sprinkler whilst Alice stands on the patio, laughing and trying to take Nell's photograph. 'Stay still,' she says.

Nell takes a small fishing net to the stream. She scoops up weed, tiny brown fish and tadpoles. Alice takes photographs of Nell with her fishing net. In one photograph, Nell is squatting down by the stream in her shorts and a vest, frowning at something in the net; in another she is lying on her tummy on the bridge.

Alice takes a photograph of Nell in the field, standing amongst the tall wheat, her arms folded across her chest. She photographs Nell at home too: Nell sitting at the kitchen table slowly eating her dinner, her spoon raised to her mouth. In another photograph Nell is sleeping, her scratched arm hanging out of the bed, eyes shut, her lips slightly parted.

Nell enjoys helping Alice develop the photographs, even if the cellar is spooky. They have to wear gloves and use special chemicals.

Alice prints her favourites and hangs them on the cottage landing. The photographs are strange because in most of them Nell is not smiling and in normal photographs the people are smiling. The photographing takes forever. They will shoot in the same spot for an hour or more and, if the photographs are not good enough, they will try again the next day, in the same place at the same time. Alice tries to explain to Nell why the photographs she has taken are not right: Nell's stance is not good, her expression is wrong, there is too much light on the wheat, or on her hair, or else there is not enough light.

Nell is patient because the photographs are important to Alice, just as her paintings are. She learned long ago about the importance of art. A lot of time must be devoted to it. 'You have to work hard to achieve anything close to good,' Alice says, adjusting the settings on the camera. 'Even harder for something great.'

September arrives. Alice paints in the mornings, and in the afternoons they go to the beach, walking for hours along the flat, deserted coastline.

Nell's hat is too big for her and she pushes it up with her gloved hand when she bends down to reach for an interesting stone. She always looks for hag stones but rarely finds any good ones.

Alice brings a bag for driftwood and Nell collects clam shells and coloured pebbles. When the tide is out she washes her wellies in the tiny streams of water that run all the way to the sea.

Beyond the watery line of the horizon there is a vertical drop to the universe below. Alice tells her this is what people used to believe about the world, that it was flat, that it must have a beginning, middle and an end, just like stories.

In the evenings, Alice stands, leaning against the doorframe, smoking, watching the sunset. She stubs her cigarettes out in an old chopped tomato tin that she leaves on the patio hidden behind a plant pot. Later, Alice will sit sideways in the armchair in the living room, her legs dangling, talking on the phone, stretching the cord from the kitchen where the cradle is fixed to the wall. Nell has to dart underneath it. 'Oh tell me about London,' Alice says dramatically to whoever is on the other end of the phone. 'It's so *quiet* here.'

The phone calls slowly cease, or at least they become

less regular. The cigarette smoking stops too. 'I don't need them,' Alice announces one morning, throwing the rest of the packet in the kitchen bin. This is how Alice makes her decisions: rashly, absolutely, without looking back.

Using the wood they collect from their long beach walks, Alice creates a small driftwood sculpture. She makes a wire frame and has a special glue that needs to be mixed in an old mug. Alice calls her figure Driftwood Man. He has a flat face and pointed chin, his arms and legs look like they might advance towards Nell in strange rigid movements. When she is finished, Alice places Driftwood Man on the narrow mantelpiece. Nell eyes him warily, checking to make sure he hasn't moved.

7

2003

On Sunday morning Scott calls and Nell finds herself giving him her address. He picks her up in his black Vauxhall Astra with the tinted windows. As Nell climbs in, she wishes she had arranged to meet Scott at a pub in town instead so she could have walked and left whenever she wanted. *Don't be silly. Sometimes you have to take risks, otherwise nothing will ever happen. This is how other people live.*

Scott glances at her. 'You look nervous.'

Nell tries to smile. 'I guess I am a little nervous. You know, getting into a strange man's car. You could be an axe murderer. You could take me into the countryside, knock me over the head with the shovel you've got in your boot, then bury me under a bush.'

Scott laughs. 'I haven't got a shovel in the boot. Luckily for you, I only keep one in there during the winter, in case of snow. Anyway, to be an axe murderer, wouldn't I have to kill you with an axe? Surely using the shovel would make me a shovel murderer?'

'I guess it would.' Nell fastens her seatbelt, taking in the bottle of half-drunk orange juice and the empty, but folded, packet of Monster Munch in the space between them.

Relax. It's just lunch.

'You don't look like the shovel-murdering type.'

Scott laughs. 'I'd love to know what he does look like.'

In the pub, a blonde-haired waitress leads them to a table for two. Nell knocks the pepper pot over and Scott rights it, catching her eye and giving her a reassuring smile.

What is this? Should I even be here? she wonders. She glances towards the pub door: a family are arriving, parents, grandparents; two children are already shaking off brightly coloured coats.

'I'm so glad you came, Nell. I wasn't sure you would.'

She sits down and so does Scott. 'Weren't you?'

'Well, I *hoped* you would. It makes a nice change. It gets a bit boring, doesn't it? Doing the same things at the weekends, seeing the same faces.'

Nell agrees. It is nice to do something different, meet new people. *This is what I should be doing. Meeting new friends. Going to new places.*

The waitress puts menus on their table and Scott rubs his hands together. He studies his menu carefully, forensically. Nell smiles. He reminds her of someone studying an exam paper, making sure they haven't missed anything.

Scott has a beer *(don't worry the food will soak it up)* and insists Nell order a glass of wine *(It's the weekend, Nell!)*. She takes a sip of wine and can feel it loosening her muscles, fuzzing the usually sharp edges of her mind. The pub is playing Norah Jones, creating a suitably ambient, relaxing Sunday atmosphere.

'Do you have family in Brighton?' she asks. 'Your parents?'

'God, no. My folks are in Bromley. It's where I grew up. I don't see much of them. Couple of times a year, you know. I've got an aunt in Rottingdean though. It's how I knew Brighton.'

'You're not close to your parents?'

Scott shrugs. 'Not really. My sister, she's done better than me. Got herself a degree, not that she's ever used it. Now she has a fella who does something with pensions. Middle management. Earns a decent wage. They've got a kid... I don't know, I guess she, my sister I mean, was always the favourite.'

Nell sympathises. 'I'm an only child but my mother's an artist. I think her art was always her favourite child.'

Scott tilts his head. 'An artist?'

'Portraits, mostly.' Nell takes a sip of wine. She feels grown-up, sitting in a pub on a Sunday, drinking chilled Sauvignon Blanc. She wonders if the waitress realises they're on a first date, or if she's taken them for a couple who have been together for years, who have dragged themselves off the sofa and out to the pub. *We should go out*, one of them would say. *Do something with the weekend. Go for lunch.* Could she be one half of a couple like that? *It's not a date*, she corrects herself, sternly.

'Your dad?' Scott asks.

'Oh, I don't know. I mean, I've never known him.'

'You've never met your dad?'

'No. Alice – my mother, she doesn't talk about him.'

'Don't you want to know?'

Nell looks down at her napkin, carefully wrapped around a shiny knife and fork. 'I did want to know, for a while. But Alice, she digs her heels in. It isn't worth upsetting her. She's always acted as if he never existed so I suppose, after a while, I did too. When I was small, I had all these ideas about him, fantasies really. But they were stupid, childish. I had nothing, no name, no photograph. I killed him.'

'You killed him?'

'My idea of him. I had to.'

Scott rubs his chin. Then the waitress appears carrying a plate in each hand and Nell is grateful for the distraction. She always feels uncomfortable talking about her father. He is nothing more than a ghost, a shadowy figure lost behind some forgotten door of her childhood imagination.

Scott is right, the food *is* good. She has chicken and he has the beef. She finishes her glass of wine and Scott flags the waitress down and orders her another, despite Nell's protests.

She learns that Scott left school at sixteen because it was never for him. For two years, he worked the telephones for a double-glazing company, cold-calling elderly women at home during *Coronation Street* and persuading them they needed new windows to keep the heat in. He was promoted and became a field salesman where he would go to pre-arranged appointments with a boot full of samples and tell the customer that the half-price offer was only on until Friday, give them a pen and show them where to sign. Since then he has worked for a second-hand car garage and a telecommunications company. Now, he manages a small sales office in Kemp Town. He has six full-time members of staff, two part-timers and a secretary.

'We sell corporate hospitality,' Scott explains. 'Boxes at Twickenham, marquees at Ascot, that sort of thing. We give them the full shebang. Champagne for breakfast, five course lunch, afternoon tea, tickets, of course. You don't have to be into sport to do the job though. My team all have scripts.'

Nell considers this. 'I suppose that's like me. I sell clothes but I'm not *that* interested in fashion. I mean, I like clothes but I'm not passionate about them.'

'You don't have to be passionate about a job, Nell,' Scott reassures her. 'You just have to pretend to be. Anyway,' he says, glancing at her, 'I think you wear nice clothes. I know I've only seen you twice now, but both times you've looked gorgeous.'

Nell can feel her cheeks reddening. She looks down at her dark jeans and the top she'd chosen to wear, the one with the apple print. She had bought both items with her work discount. She watches Scott stabbing two large parsnips with his fork then imagines him at work, managing his office, holding team meetings, writing sales figures on a whiteboard, instructing his secretary to photocopy documents and buying doughnuts for his team on a Friday.

'Tell me more about your job.'

Scott swallows, leans back in his chair. 'It's mostly cold calling. We don't get much repeat business. Sometimes the hospitality suites we provide aren't actually on site. They're always close by though. You know, a hotel down the road or something, but some clients get funny about that.' Scott shrugs. 'It's all in the small print.'

Nell pushes several potatoes and the rest of the red cabbage to the side of her plate. She feels full.

'So what do you like to do, Nell, when you're not working?'

'Read.' She hesitates. 'And I sometimes write things: poems, short stories.'

Scott raises an eyebrow. 'Stories? Maybe you could write one about me? The shovel murderer who has no shovel.' He laughs at his own joke, puts his knife and fork together on his spotless plate then leans back in his chair. 'I'm afraid I don't read much. I'm more of a TV man.'

'We all like different things.'

'That's very true, Nell.'

She looks down at her napkin in her lap.

'Do you have a boyfriend? Are you seeing anyone?'

'No. The girls at work, they're always saying I should go out. Date.'

'Well, what do you think?'

Nell folds the corners of her napkin. 'I think... I don't know.'

Scott smiles but says nothing. He beckons to the waitress and asks for the bill. He insists on paying, producing a wad of twenties from his wallet and leaving a generous tip. On the drive home Nell feels tired, not just sleepy but a huge, unexpected, wave of exhaustion. She puts it down to the wine. She isn't used to it. The clouds have gathered over the downs and it begins to rain, a light spring rain that makes the countryside look greener, fresher. She glances at Scott, his hands on the wheel. She has forgotten what it feels like for someone else to do something for her, even if it is only driving.

Back in town, they have left the rain behind. It's late in the afternoon and Nell decides that, once home, she will grab her mac in case the rain returns and walk along the beach. She needs to clear her head. Scott pulls up outside the gate and Nell undoes her seatbelt.

'There's something I need to tell you, Nell. There's something I don't think you know about me. I'm worried that if I tell you, you won't ever want to see me again but I feel that if I don't, it isn't fair on you. You should know.'

She thinks about making a joke. Maybe Scott is in a religious cult. Perhaps he works for MI5 and the sales manager job is a cover. She is about to say something silly but stops when she sees his face.

'Scott. What is it?'

'I've got a prosthetic leg.'

Nell wasn't sure what she was expecting him to say but it certainly wasn't that.

'I didn't notice.'

'Most people don't.'

'Have you always had it?'

'No. I was in an accident when I was fifteen. I got out of a car without looking and another car smashed into us and took the door off, almost my leg too. They couldn't save it. I had a below-knee amputation. I've had the prosthetic, now, almost as long as I didn't have it. I mean, it's all I've known for a long time. But I realise it's weird for people. I'm not sure if you noticed – the car's an automatic. I've still got my right leg.'

'I'm so sorry,' she says slowly, considerately. 'That's

awful. But it shouldn't make any difference to the way people see you. You shouldn't be afraid to tell people.'

'Thank you.'

'I had a nice time this afternoon. Really, I did. You shouldn't worry about what people think.' Nell puts her hand on the door handle but, before she has a chance to open the door, Scott leans over and kisses her on the lips. The kiss takes Nell by surprise. She gives herself to it. She does not want to offend or reject Scott. She feels a panic rising in her chest and then the feeling that she is slipping away, liquifying. *It's just a kiss. Don't pull back. He'll think you're weird. He's a nice guy. Take a chance on this.*

When Scott releases Nell he smiles and runs a hand through his hair. 'Wow.'

'Mm.' Nell nods because it feels appropriate.

'That was really something.' Scott places his hands on the wheel. He's staring into the courtyard. He turns to her. 'I wanted you. As soon as I saw you in the pub.' Scott shakes his head. 'I don't know, Nell. It was like the whole room just stopped and you were all I could see.'

She says nothing, bites her lip. She isn't sure how she feels. She doesn't want to upset Scott's fragile self-esteem.

'Would you mind if we went out one evening this week?'

Scott looks so hopeful Nell can't bear to say no. 'Yes,' she says, opening the car door. 'Yes, that would be fine. Thank you for lunch,' she adds.

'I'll call,' Scott says. 'Soon.'

When Nell enters the house she closes the door behind her and leans against it, listening to the car pull away. When she is sure he has gone, she goes into the kitchen and pours herself a glass of water. Her hand is shaking. *Why are you being like this? Don't mess this up like you mess everything up.* She puts her glass in the sink, steps into the hallway, grabs her rain mac from the peg rail and opens the front door.

8

Scott slips easily into Nell's life. At the weekends, he often appears outside the shop just as Nell is finishing work. 'Thought you might want to grab some food,' he'll say.

It seems only polite when Scott has made the effort to come into town to meet her. She has never eaten out so often in her life.

Nell spends less time at the house and more of her evenings at Scott's place, sitting on his slippery leather sofa watching his large flatscreen TV.

Scott's flat is on the fifth floor in a new development overlooking the marina in Shoreham-by-Sea. 'It's got the same view as the penthouse,' Scott had told her. 'Only there's less windows to clean, and I saved myself twenty grand. I needed a place with a lift. It broke down once. I should have sued them.'

Everything in Scott's flat is shiny and functional but somehow, she thinks, soulless. There are no books, just a glass-fronted DVD cabinet. 'There are three hundred DVDs in there. I've got all the *Rocky* films,' Scott said proudly. 'The full set.'

A blue photographic print of a London skyline hangs

on the wall above the sofa; there's a *Reservoir Dogs* poster in the bathroom.

'I saved for five years for the deposit for this place. Every fucking penny. Twenty-four grand in five years.'

She agrees that this is admirable.

'Most kids nowadays get everything handed to them on a plate. It's always the bank of Mum and Dad. We don't live in a society that values hard work, Nell. That's the problem.'

Nell is never sure what to say to when Scott gets worked up about things like this. There must be, she supposes, some truth to what he says.

If she isn't at his flat, Scott calls her in the evenings to ask about her day, and tell her about his. She finds it difficult to understand why someone else would be so interested in the boring trivialities of her life. She keeps expecting Scott to disappear as quickly as he appeared. One day, she thinks, he won't call, but that day never arrives.

When Nell is with Scott she experiences an odd rush of adrenaline, a sharpening of her senses that makes her chest tighten and her breath quicken. She doesn't know if this adrenaline is good or bad, but at least it is something.

She isn't sure, when she looks back several months after meeting Scott, how or when the sex began. She struggles to remember a defining romantic moment. The sex happened because it was always going to happen. She realises she probably knew this all along, from that first Sunday lunch.

Scott has sex with Nell several times a week. Nell knows what is required of her and does her best to meet these requirements. She does not enjoy the sex and this, she decides, is further confirmation that she is not normal. She knows she is supposed to enjoy sex. At first she tries hard to pretend but after a while she realises Scott doesn't care. Whatever is going on in his head does not seem to relate to her. She feels her body could be anyone's and, in a way, that makes things easier. She lets her mind go blank and waits until it's over.

At first she wondered if an unconscious part of her felt a repulsion because of Scott's leg, which he always removes before they go to bed. She is fairly sure though, that she would feel the same about the sex if Scott had both his legs. Still, she feels guilty. *I am a terrible person. I am a terrible, superficial person because I don't enjoy sex with a less able-bodied person.*

Nell understands that relationships are transactional. She must endure the sex if she is to be with Scott, if she is not to be lonely, if she is to have someone in her life who loves and cares about her as Scott tells her he does. Not only does Scott tell Nell he loves her, he tells her, often, that they are meant to be together.

They were walking along East Street together one

Sunday afternoon. It was during those first few weeks, before the sex began. Sitting at a small table in the centre of the pedestrianised street was a woman wearing a purple headscarf and rings with stones of different colours. The sign on the table read: *Fortune Telling, Five pounds.* Nell had looked curiously at the woman, who had smiled at her.

'Do you believe in any of that?' Scott asked.

'I don't think so.'

Scott had looked thoughtful. 'Well,' he'd said. 'I didn't believe in any of that until…' He'd trailed off, his gaze fixed on something across the street.

'Until what?' Nell asked, gently.

Scott looked down at the pavement. 'Oh, you'll think I'm a dick.'

'No, I won't. You can tell me.'

Scott breathed out heavily through his nostrils. 'I saw a fortune teller at a fête once. I was only fourteen. The summer before I lost my leg. My sister dared me.' He paused, rubbed the back of his neck. 'It sounds crazy but I could tell right away she was the real deal. The way she looked at me, it was weird. It was like she *knew* me. She touched my hand and read my palm.'

'What did she say?' Nell asked, tentatively, fearing something awful.

Scott exhaled deeply again. 'She said I would meet someone very special in my thirty-first year, that I would know as soon as I met this person that she would be the one, that I was *destined* to be with her. "It's written for you," she said. Those were her exact words. I can still hear them now. All these years later. This is why I *know* we're meant to be together. I knew as soon as I saw you that you were the one she told me about. I know it like I know the sky is blue today. I've never felt like this before, about anyone.'

Nell had looked at the sky, more grey than blue but she knew that wasn't the point.

Scott reached for her hand and she'd let him take it. She felt somewhat taken aback by the strength of Scott's feelings for her, and by how sure he was about it all. Nell had never felt that sure about anything. Perhaps that was another of her deficiencies. Other people seemed to know what job they should be doing, or where they should live, or who they should be in a relationship with. It was easier to let other people make the decisions, people who knew the things that she did not.

Once a week Scott visits his elderly aunt, Joan, who lives in a bungalow in Rottingdean with a Yorkshire terrier called Dennis. Nell tags along on these visits. 'She doesn't have anyone else,' Scott tells her.

Nell decides that Scott's weekly visits to Joan make him a kind and caring person. He may not be close to his parents but he clearly cares about his aunt.

74

'Are you sure Joan wouldn't prefer to see just you?'

'She likes you. She wants to see me with someone. She wants to see me happy.'

So Nell finds herself sitting in the front room of Joan's bungalow, drinking sherry, whilst Joan and Scott chain-smoke and Dennis twitches in his sleep by the two-bar fire with its fake orange glow. On the walls are photographs of Joan's deceased terriers, the ones that pre-date Dennis. Joan has a drinks cabinet, Scott's old TV, and a collection of small cats of different sizes that look like they have been stolen from the windows of Chinese restaurants. Nell has never asked about the cats.

'I'm so glad you've taken him on,' Joan says, emerging from the downstairs loo one evening. Nell is on her way to the kitchen to fetch the sherry glasses. Joan stands very close to Nell, scrutinising her. Joan's voice is dry and raspy, a smoker's voice. She smells like fermented fruit: sweet and musty.

'Yes,' Nell says even though she isn't sure 'taking on' Scott was ever her intention. They return to the living room where Scott is eating a cheese sandwich Joan made for him. Nell usually passes on the sandwiches. The bread is often stale because a whole loaf is too much for Joan to eat in a week; the cheese is pre-sliced and rubbery. Alice used to say margarine was one molecule away from plastic.

'She should eat more,' Scott says, gesturing towards Nell and taking a bite of his sandwich.

Joan rests her cigarette in the cut-glass ashtray on the side table and squints at Nell. 'She's a little doll,' she says, with no indication as to whether this is a compliment or a criticism.

The conversation moves on to plans for the conservatory Joan wants built on the back of the bungalow.

'They aren't half slow getting back to me,' Joan says. 'I'll be dead before they finish it.'

'Don't be ridiculous,' Scott replies. 'I'll have a word with them. I know how to handle these people.'

'Well, I'll be happy if I get a year out of it,' Joan says thoughtfully, blowing a cloud of smoke in the direction of the TV.

'You're too skinny,' Scott tells Nell later in the car. 'It makes you look ill. Anyone would think you're a vegetarian.'

'I do eat quite a lot,' Nell says. 'I've just always been slim.'

Scott shakes his head. Once his opinion is decided on something he is unmoving. 'You'll feel better if you eat more. Besides,' he adds, smiling to himself, 'It'll give me more to get hold of in the bedroom.'

Nell feels her shoulder muscles stiffen. She says nothing.

Scott sighs and closes the window. 'Maybe you should try and wear looser fitting clothes. That way you won't look so skinny, and so young.'

Nell looks out of the window, at the flat grey sea and disappearing sun. In half an hour it will be fully dark.

It isn't the first time Scott has made comments about her appearance. Last weekend, when Nell stayed over at the flat, she'd emerged from the shower wrapped in a towel, her hair wet. She'd gone straight into the bedroom where she'd left her rucksack and began applying moisturiser to her skin. With the towel wrapped around her, she had become conscious of Scott watching her. She could see his reflection in the wardrobe's mirrored door.

'You look like a little rat when your hair's wet,' Scott had said. 'Little ratty face. That's what I'll call you from now on.'

Nell thought at first she'd misheard him. 'What?' she'd said, turning, whilst trying to hold up the towel. But Scott only grinned and walked away, leaving Nell staring at her reflection in the wardrobe mirror. *He's joking,* she reminded herself. *He's just joking with you. Lighten up. Don't be so sensitive.*

9

1993

Alice has decided Nell should go to school so she can make friends and learn how to do maths. The children have to line up, one by one, in the playground outside their classroom. Parents hover nearby. This is Nell's first day but for the others they are simply returning to a new year, new classrooms and a new teacher.

When they'd arrived, Nell had held onto the sleeve of Alice's jumper, stretching the material, not wanting to join the other children. Alice had led her over and found her a place in the line. Now, Alice stands over by the fence. Nell already knows that Alice will never join the huddle of parents, fuss, make small talk with the other mothers and occasional father.

She waits in line, her rucksack on her back, clutching the P.E. bag Alice made from an old pillowcase. The children are beginning to move forward, into their classroom. She turns and searches for Alice but she is no longer there.

Nell is to sit with Rachel as their names are next to

78

each other in the register. Eleonora Mae and Rachel Nunnally. Rachel says the hairdresser told her she should brush her hair at least fifty strokes every morning to make it shiny. Nell rarely brushes her hair because Alice says you shouldn't brush curls. Nell has never been to a hairdresser. Alice cuts her hair for her over the kitchen sink using nail scissors. They put the cut hair outside in the garden so the birds can have it for their nests.

After they have been shown their tables, trays and pegs, all the children sit cross-legged on the carpet whilst Mrs Reed writes sums on the whiteboard. Nell prays not to be picked. She does not know the answers. It is difficult to keep her thoughts in the classroom. They are in the playground, along the road, in a country she has not yet visited, or in a book she is reading. It is strange that there is a whole world out there, yet she has to sit on one small patch of carpet in front of squiggles and symbols that don't seem to be anything to do with her.

In the afternoon they have art and are allowed to paint. School is full of rules she is frightened of breaking. There are rules about where to sit, where to hang your bag, and about putting up your hand before you speak. You are supposed to go to the toilet at break and lunchtimes but you can ask to go during class time if you are desperate. The toilet roll is thin and crispy, like tracing paper. At lunch, Nell overheard a small, freckled girl with bunches and shiny hair clips whisper to her friend that they are only allowed to use one square. Is this true? How would they know? Do the teachers check the toilet roll to see how many squares have been used for each wee?

Nell wonders if there are rules about painting pictures too. Rachel hands Nell a piece of slippery paper. 'This one is for you.' And then, as if reading Nell's mind, 'Mrs Reed says we can paint whatever we like because today is the first day.'

She watches Rachel dip her paintbrush into the red and draw four lines that make a square.

'What is it?'

'It's my house. You can paint yours if you like. I might paint a horse called Clover because I've always wanted a horse called Clover.'

Nell paints her own house, Grandma's cottage. She does not paint a garage and a porch with steps like Rachel because her house does not have a garage or a porch. Next to the cottage, Nell paints herself and Alice, one big stick person and one smaller stick person. They stand holding hands and smiling. Nell paints a yellow sun and, at the top of her paper, a blue line of sky, just like Rachel has. Grandma, she thinks, can't be in the painting because she is no longer here.

Nell begins to paint the tiles on the roof of the cottage. Starting in one corner she paints lots of tiny rectangles.

'That's very good,' Rachel says approvingly, 'but doing the roof of your house like that will take you forever.'

Nell notices many of the girls in the classroom have painted their houses, or their families. Some have painted the sea, sun and sky: a wavy blue line at the bottom of the paper and a straight blue line at the top with a sun in the middle and a boat in the water. The boys have drawn cars and tractors, except for one boy with a runny nose called Robbie Lock who has drawn a woman dancing.

At three o'clock, Alice collects her. Nell says school was okay but she would prefer not to go again.

'See how you feel tomorrow,' Alice says.

After school, Nell needs time to come back to herself. She sits on her bed tracing the grain of the wood on the headboard along to the knot, looking for the familiar scratches. She wraps her arms tightly around her knees and rocks a little, back and forth, until Alice calls her for dinner. She needs to forget the squeaking of chairs, the clattering of trays, the laughter in the playground, the questions she doesn't understand.

Downstairs, she takes the picture from her bag and shows Alice.

'Why have you painted the sky like that?'

What does Alice mean?

'That is not how the sky is.' Alice reaches for her paints and an easel. She gives Nell a piece of paper and a brush. 'Come on,' she says. 'Put your wellies on.'

They walk to the field at the back of the cottage, Alice carrying the easel, Nell holding the paints and palette.

When Alice has found the right spot she tells Nell to look at the sky.

'Paint what's really there,' she says. 'See how the sky goes all the way to the ground?'

Nell is cold and tired from her first day at school. She does not want to be standing in a field, painting.

'And look,' Alice says. 'The sky isn't just blue. It's grey and white.'

Nell mixes black and white to make grey. She tries to paint the sky as Alice wants her to paint it. She preferred her own sky because it was the same as everybody else's.

Each morning they have an assembly. The children line up in register order and are led into the hall where they must sit in rows on the shiny floor. There is a smell of fresh polish, and the rectangular slats that fit together to form a continuous, comforting pattern.

As the children file in, classical music plays from two speakers above the small stage. A projector tells them, each day, which piece they are listening to: *Winter*, Vivaldi; *Jupiter*, Holst or *The Flight of the Bumblebee*, Rimsky-Korsakov. The unfamiliar names of the composers remind Nell of the names on the spines of Alice's art and photography books.

In assembly you have to sit cross-legged with a straight back but Nell notices many slumped and curved ones.

She tries to keep her own as straight as possible because that is the rule.

On Friday, a teacher brings in a fish tank full of water. She says the water in the tank is the same amount of water wasted if they do not turn the tap off whilst brushing their teeth. It is important not to waste water because of the children in Africa who have to walk many miles each day to find a well. They are asked to donate clothes for the African children. Nell donates her old Snoopy T-shirt. Every time she brushes her teeth she thinks of the girl in Africa, the same age as her, walking for many miles with a pot on her head, wearing her Snoopy T-shirt.

Nell finds that in spelling and reading she is better than the other children. 'But I've read this one,' she says quietly when she is given her reading homework. 'But you can't have read all of them,' Mrs Reed says, so Nell learns to say nothing. Her spelling may be above average but her handwriting is apparently poor, and she doesn't hold her pencil in the right way. 'Like this,' Mrs Reed says, placing Nell's fingers along the groves of the fat triangular pencil.

Before P.E. they have to change into their kits at their tables. Nell takes all her clothes off. She stands, naked, rummaging around in her pillowcase P.E bag to see what she is supposed to wear.

'What are you doing?' Rachel whispers to her.

'What do you mean?'

'You're not supposed to be naked. You don't get changed like that. You keep your knickers and vest on.'

Nell looks around the classroom. None of the other children are naked. Some of them are staring at her. Others have begun to giggle.

'Look at Eleonora. She's *naked*,' the girl with the shiny hair clips says, pointing at Nell.Mrs Reed looks surprised and Nell realises she has got it wrong. It is not okay to be naked at school. She quickly puts her knickers on and finds her vest.

At home, Nell asks Alice why the other children give envelopes of money to their teacher on a Monday morning.

'Time for school dinner collection,' Mrs Reed tells them.

All the children that have school dinners go to their bags and produce their envelopes. All except Nell and Robbie Lock, who everyone knows lives with people who aren't his real parents. They know this because Robbie's mother turned up at the school gates one day crying and shouting and Mrs Reed had to go and make a phone call. Robbie Lock wears a plain blue jumper instead of a real school jumper with the correct school logo. The other boys make fun of him for this, along with his snotty nose. Last week, in the playground at break time, Nell heard two of the boys in her class teasing Robbie. *There's Robbie*

*Snot. Why don't you have a real school jumper? Hey, if you
lick the spit off my hand I'll give you 20p.*

Nell glanced at Robbie and watched him thinking it
over. *Don't.*

'Oh, you don't have to worry about that,' Alice tells
her, when Nell mentions the dinner money envelope. 'I
filled in that form, remember?'

Alice then decides Nell can take a packed lunch two
days a week. She gives Nell thick cheese sandwiches with
homemade pickles or a tub of herbs and salad leaves from
the garden. Sometimes there are flowers; blue chicory or
purple chive heads. Alice often makes salads from the
garden for dinner. They eat these salads with the pigeon
breasts a man Alice knows called Pete-from-the-pub sells
to her. Pete-from-the-pub shoots pigeons and catches
crayfish. Alice gives him vegetables from the garden in
exchange for the pigeon breasts. When Pete-from-the-
pub comes over, Alice offers him coffee, sometimes beer.
Nell watches all this warily, keeping an eye on things. She
doesn't like men in the cottage, men who linger. She only
liked Mike who has a life in London and wouldn't live
with a woman in that way.

She often wonders about her father in America. Is
he like the American fathers on television? Does he go
surfing, carry a brown bag of shopping under his arm,
keep his eggs in the fridge? She imagines him tall, tanned,
wearing deck shoes. Her father is not a subject she can

discuss with Alice. Any questions about his whereabouts have always resulted in a sigh, a frown, a quick brush off.

'She's eating flowers,' a boy at Nell's lunch table says, loudly, pointing at Nell's lunch.

His friend looks over. 'They're *weeds*,' he says. 'You can't eat them.'

'Yes, you can.' Nell feels her cheeks turning pink.

Rachel looks over at the two boys. 'Shut up,' she says. 'You eat bogies.'

Part Two

10

2003

One evening, when Robyn and Kelly-Ann are both out, Nell invites Scott into the house for a cup of tea. She suggests they stay in the kitchen so Scott doesn't have to do the stairs but Scott is adamant he wants to see Nell's room. He climbs them, slowly and steadily, and Nell feels guilty with every step.

Standing in the doorway of her tiny bedroom, he frowns at the single bed, hanging rail and inherited Rothko print. 'This is it?'

'Yes.'

They move into the living area. Scott stares at the worn blue carpet and sagging sofa with the mismatched cushions and faded throws. He glances disdainfully at the giraffe.

'It's a shithole. Come and live with me.'

A week later, Nell is packing up her belongings.

Kelly-Ann had hugged her. 'I'll see you both in the pub, sometime.'

'Of course,' Nell had said, although she'd known this

unlikely. She hasn't introduced Scott to Kelly-Ann yet. Somehow the timing has never been right.

Only Robyn has seen Scott. She caught a glimpse of him, a few weeks ago, as he waited outside the courtyard for Nell one evening.

'Is that him?' Robyn had asked, from the balcony where she was smoking.

'That's him.'

'Hm.'

The night before she leaves, Robyn appears in the doorway of Nell's room. Nell is busy rolling clothes on the bed, stuffing them into a rucksack.

'Are you sure about this?'

Nell looks up. 'Yes. Of course.'

'You barely know him.'

Nell's cheeks flush. *What has this got to do with Robyn?*

'And you haven't been here long. You can't always run, Nell.'

She glares at Robyn, her nostrils flared. 'I'm not *running*. I'm moving in with someone, building a life. I'm doing the opposite of running.'

Robyn doesn't look convinced. 'You don't think, Nell…'

'Think what?'

'That maybe you're looking for your father?'

Nell breathes out deeply, lifts her chin. 'Thank you for

your insight but no, I am not looking for my father. I have *never* looked for my father.'

'Because you shouldn't, Nell. And running, it won't help.'

'Help with what?' she snaps.

'With looking for him, or for yourself.'

Nell rolls her eyes, and Robyn holds her hands up, a defensive gesture. 'Alright, I won't say any more.'

'Please, don't.' Nell shakes her head, reaches for a pair of jeans.

After Robyn leaves, Nell listens to her footsteps ascending the stairs followed by the click of her bedroom door opening, then closing. Nell sits on her bed in the blue twilight of the evening. She hadn't wanted to part from Robyn like that, but what gives Robyn the right to comment on Nell's decisions, to speak about her father? Robyn doesn't even *know* her. They shared a house; a bathroom, a kettle, a door mat. As Robyn had made clear, they do not even do film or fondue nights. Nell shakes her head, grabs a handful of hangers and shoves them into a plastic bag.

The following day, she drags everything she owns into the living room whilst she hoovers and cleans her room, leaving it as she found it, making sure she gets her deposit back. The room seems to have already given her up. It's ready for its new occupant, whoever that will be.

Scott arrives, beeping his horn in the courtyard. Nell

puts her possessions, stuffed into supermarket bags-for-life, in the boot of Scott's Astra, making several trips up and down the stairs whilst Scott stays by the car. Her washing basket is shoved onto the back seat. When she's put everything into the car, Scott drives them over to the flat. In celebration, he orders a Chinese takeaway and buys Nell a bunch of pale pink carnations. She doesn't have a vase, and neither does Scott, so she puts them in a pint glass.

'We'll be able to live much more cost-effectively now you're here with me,' Scott tells her, later that evening, when she is crushing the empty takeaway cartons into the recycling bag.

In fact, the opposite proves to be true. Scott decides that Nell must contribute to his mortgage which means she must pay half. He helps her to set up a monthly direct debit from her account to his. She must contribute to the bills too, especially the water as her showers are longer than his. Although they agree to split the bills, the final reminders pile up in the kitchen, on top of the microwave, and Nell ends up calling the companies and paying them herself. It is easier than asking Scott, who always seems to have something more important to do. Scott is at work during the week but Nell has at least one weekday off. He tells her to go the supermarket because it is too busy at the weekends so Nell ends up paying for the weekly shop too. She finds she is worse off than when she rented her room. She never has anything left at the end of the month. Not that it matters. She doesn't have much to spend her salary on. There is rarely anything she needs for herself. She buys books from the charity shops; she has a uniform allowance, and a generous discount at work for clothes.

Weeks can often pass before Nell realises she hasn't returned Alice's calls. The calls seem pointless anyway. Neither of them ever have any news and they are both hopeless at small talk. Now, however, she does have news; she's been living with Scott for over a month. She calls Alice from Scott's flat as she has a day off and Scott is at work. It's the middle of the afternoon. Nell knows Alice is more likely to answer the phone in the evening when she isn't working but she doesn't want to disturb Scott by making a phone call when he's watching TV. Neither does she want to give Scott an excuse to talk about Alice.

Nell knows there are lots of way in which she is inadequate: her size, her looks, her age and, according to Scott, her lack of experience about the ways of the world. Scott has formed his own opinions of Nell's childhood. He likes to use words like mollycoddled, stuck-up, and spoiled. He sneaks these words in, like little pinpricks.

'You think you're so fucking great, don't you?' Scott had said to her last weekend. 'Just because Mummy's an artist you think you can have all the fancy ideas.'

Nell was in the process of filling the washing machine. She'd paused, a pair of Scott's tracksuit bottoms in her hands. 'I don't have any ideas,' she'd said.

Scott had grunted and turned away from her.

'It's people like your mother who abuse the system,' he liked to say. 'People who think they're better than everyone else. "I'll just stay at home and paint whilst all you other fuckers go to work." Lazy bastards.'

She'd told him how Alice taught evening and weekend classes at the local college, and life drawing from home. Whatever she said only seemed to further enrage Scott. Half the time she had no idea what Scott was talking about or what exactly it was she had done wrong. When Nell mentioned, one evening, that she would prefer to go into the bedroom and read than sit and watch the car show Scott was watching, he leapt up from the sofa and shouted at her. 'Oh, I'm so fucking sorry this isn't good enough for you. I forget that you're used to sitting around in the evening drinking port from the fucking *bureau*.'

'I don't know what you mean.'

Nell couldn't always work out what it was about her, and Alice, that made Scott so cross. All she knew was that it was better to sit and watch TV with Scott, and to read on her lunch breaks and days off, or when Scott fell asleep on the sofa. He had made it clear he didn't want Nell's books 'cluttering up the place' so she keeps her books under the bed, or at work in her locker, or else

94

she takes them back to the charity shop when she has finished with them.

A few weeks after she'd moved in, Scott had asked about her father again. He'd been lying on the sofa drinking a can of larger. He'd had too much. Nell knew, now, not to take anything to heart that Scott said when he'd had too much to drink.

'Scarper then, did he?' Scott had asked of her father. 'When she was pregnant?'

'I don't really know.' Nell had tried to keep her voice calm and even. 'Alice told me once that he was in America but it wasn't true. It was just something she said.'

This had been the wrong thing to say as it had worked Scott up. 'Lying bitch! Imagine telling a kid something like that!'

'I don't think she meant it to hurt me. She probably thought I'd forget. I was quite young. It was just something to say, like when you tell a child that by the time they're older the doctors will have invented a pill which will mean people can live forever.'

'Bollocks. No one ever told me that. It's child abuse, that's what it is. So where is he then?' He adjusted his position on the sofa, trying to get his leg comfortable.

'I don't know. I don't want to know.'

'Too right. Bastard.'

Nell had wanted to add that she had no idea if her father had even known Alice was pregnant, that she didn't know anything about the circumstances as Alice never wanted to talk about them. Instead, she'd kept quiet, not wanting to prolong the conversation.

On the phone Alice tells Nell about the closure of the village post office, how high the river is after the recent rain and about the heron she saw in the garden last Thursday and then again on Monday. 'He must live over on the wetlands,' Alice says. 'I've called him Frank.'

'I've moved in with my boyfriend.'

'Oh,' Alice says. She pauses. 'I'm glad you're happy.'

'Yes.'

'I hope to meet him sometime.'

'Mm,' Nell says, thinking it unlikely.

'How's your job?'

'Fine.'

'Are you writing?'

'No, why?'

'You used to. That English teacher of yours was always telling me you should write.'

Nell frowns. 'I'm quite busy.'

'As long as you're okay.'

'I'll give you a call next week.' She won't. It's more likely to be another three weeks, or longer.

'Okay,' Alice says, and then, 'have fun.'

This, Nell realises, is what Alice thinks she is doing in Brighton. Having fun. Nell knows that she's not having fun yet she isn't sure what to do about it. When she leaves the shop for the evening, Scott will be there, waiting for her. She'll be locking up with Teresa and one of the others. Scott will give the girls his dimpled smile and ask how they all are. 'He's lovely, your boyfriend,' the girls say, and Nell isn't sure why Scott has picked her. She supposes she should try to be happy. She thinks of all she has: her job, her colleagues, Scott's flat, her relationship. She has made a life for herself. It isn't perfect but surely it is something to be grateful for.

11

They are on their way home from work one evening when Scott stops at the garage for petrol. He insists on dropping Nell off at work and picking her up whenever he can. If Nell's shift starts at eight thirty, or finishes at six, he likes them to travel in or home together. If Nell takes the bus to work, Scott always texts her to make sure she made it in safely which she thinks caring of him. Nell actually wouldn't mind getting the bus every day but Scott won't hear of it. 'What kind of man would I be if I let you take the bus when I could drop you? Anyway, I don't like you taking the bus. You never know who might talk to you. All the nutters take the bus.'

She thinks of the way she used to feel anxious when a man sat next to her on the bus and realises that Scott is only being kind, taking care of her. Despite this, she can't help missing those daily walks along the front, her bus rides to Devil's Dyke or the other side of town. Other than when she is at work, she is rarely without Scott. She supposes it must be the same for all couples.

There's a queue at the garage. Nell can see Scott,

through the windows, holding two packets of crisps. She picks up the newspaper in the footwell. Scott often buys a paper on his way to work.

Nell turns the pages idly until she reaches the culture section. *RADA scholarship student lands big role.* Beneath the headline is a picture of Robbie Lock. She scans the article, smiles. Robert is to play George Emerson in a new film adaptation of *A Room with a View*.

She thinks of that day: the frost on the fields, the icy puddles. On her way out, the pharmacist calling at her to wait, she'd bumped straight into Robbie. He'd been on his way in to pick up a prescription for his granddad who he was then living with. They'd sat on the bench by the pond and she'd told him what had happened.

Scott opens the car door and climbs in.

'Look,' she says, showing him the newspaper.

Scott glances at the article whilst shoving the key into the ignition. 'What?'

'I went to school with Robbie.'

Scott studies the photograph. 'Close, were you?'

Nell looks again at Robbie's smiling face. She never spoke to him much after that day at the hospital. She had felt too embarrassed, too ashamed.

'He was kind to me,' she says finally.

Scott laughs. 'Sleep with him, did you?'

'No. I didn't.'

'I bet you did.'

Nell shakes her head. 'Scott... No, it wasn't like that.' She thinks of what Darren had said about Robbie and Niko. 'He was gay.'

'I've heard that one before.'

'I didn't sleep with him.'

Scott makes a grunting noise and starts the engine. 'Well, you'd better not get in touch with him now. He'll think you're after his money.'

Nell closes the newspaper and puts it back in the footwell. 'I won't get in touch with him now.'

'Good,' Scott says. 'Let's get a bottle of wine in for tonight. We can toast your ex-boyfriend.'

'I thought you could cook?' Scott says, six weeks after Nell moves in.

It's late in the evening. The new season's stock arrived today which involved a complete floor and window change. Teresa left Nell a handover in the office. *Hi, hun. Follow the guidelines on the intranet. And please don't do anything fancy in the window. All the shops are supposed to look the same. Send the time sheets and take the rubbish out (please!). I didn't get time to do it. Thanks! T x.*

Two of the girls, Molly and Becky, are new. It's Molly's first week and she can barely work the till. Nell spent her day supervising the new girls, giving out floor-move instructions, stripping mannequins, wheeling rails of stock to the front of the shop. At lunch, she sat in the office completing the payroll sheets Teresa should have sent yesterday.

'You'll run yourself ragged at this rate,' Shirley, the part-timer, remarked as Nell rushed past her, her arms full of dresses still in plastic.

Shirley has been at the shop nine years, longer than any of them. Nell gets the feeling that Shirley doesn't need to work, that she only comes in for the gossip and the discount.

'Oh, it's alright,' Nell had said.

Shirley frowned. 'They should be paying you the assistant manager's salary. You look knackered.'

'Honestly, Shirley. It keeps me busy. I hate it when it's quiet and there's nothing to do but space the hangers.'

Shirley tried to smile but her forehead creased. 'Hmmm.'

Later, when Nell was in the office at lunch doing the time sheets, Shirley had poked her head around the door. 'Brought you a cuppa, love.' She set the mug down next to the mouse mat and opened the plastic tub she'd been carrying under her arm. 'And a slice of cake. I made a banana loaf yesterday. I left the tub on the tea-room table for the girls but I'm not sure you saw it. Didn't want you to miss out. There's a few bits left.'

Nell reached for a piece of cake. 'Thank you.'

Shirley paused by the door. 'How's that boyfriend of

yours? Hope he'll run you a hot bath tonight after the day you've had.'

'He's fine,' she'd said, and then, 'Sorry Shirley, I'd better get on.'

Shirley looked like she wanted to say something else but nodded instead. She closed the door behind her as she left.

Now, Nell is sitting across the table from Scott, waiting for him to finish with the pepper. Scott always has a lot of pepper. He covers everything he eats in a layer of grey powder. She made pasta with tomato sauce and vegetables because she didn't get home until eight and there wasn't much in.

'All we have is pasta. Can't you do anything else?'

This isn't true. Last night she cooked chicken with new potatoes and green beans. She would like to remind him but she doesn't. She has come to learn that defending her actions, when Scott is in one of his moods, only makes matters worse.

Scott slams his fist against the table and Nell jumps.

'Are you even listening to me?'

She looks at Scott, blinking slowly, her fork half-way to her mouth.

'I said, I'm fucking sick of pasta.'

He sweeps his plate off the table and onto the cream carpet, leaving a trail of vegetables and peas. He stands and breaths in deeply. 'I'm going for a cigarette.'

Nell waits until she hears the front door slam. She looks at her own, untouched, dinner in front of her. She sits there for a moment, her shoulders slumped. In the kitchen, she scrapes the dinner into the bin. She tears off a wad of kitchen paper, then takes it, along with a damp sponge, into the living area. Kneeling, she begins to scoop up the sauce.

Scott returns a short while later. He says nothing about Nell's attempts to clean the carpet. She will have to buy carpet cleaner although she is sure it will be stained for good.

Scott sits on the sofa, his head in his hands. 'I'm sorry.'

Nell stands in the kitchen doorway, a sauce-stained tea towel in her hands. 'It's okay.'

'Dina's handed her notice in. I've got a client kicking off because the marquee wasn't on site. My leg's giving me shit.'

'It's fine,' Nell says again, because she wants it to be. She should have listened. It doesn't matter. She knows, now, he isn't keen on pasta.

12

1993

Rachel takes Nell under her wing. This is what Alice tells her. 'It's nice that girl has taken you under her wing.' Rachel has always wanted a younger sister, someone she can try out new hairstyles on, or make a den with under the slide. They are both only-children but Rachel has two parents who live together instead of just one. Rachel tells her, quite frankly one day, when they are by the climbing frame, that her mummy had other babies in her tummy but they all died. Nell wonders if Mrs Nunnally buried the babies in the garden and placed daffodils over the graves as she and Alice did for the baby bird, or if they slid into the wall like Grandma.

Mr Nunnally is a vet. He has to put his hand up cows' bottoms, Rachel tells her. When Mr Nunnally collects Rachel from school one afternoon Nell looks at his hands and wonders which one he uses for this purpose.

Mrs Nunnally is a teacher but her job is in a different school, further away, so Rachel's nana collects her from school and looks after her until Mrs Nunnally arrives home.

Rachel suggests that Nell should come over to her house after school. Alice is pleased because this means she will have more time to work. Nell and Rachel watch cartoons and Rachel's nana offers them milky tea, and toast with homemade marmalade. Rachel and Nell pick the bits out and leave them at the side of their plates.

Nell realises that people live in different ways and have different things in their homes. The curtains and cushions in Rachel's living room all match. The pictures on the walls are of men and women kissing, or holding umbrellas, or else the pictures are of vegetables. The Nunnallys don't have one cupboard of mismatched plates and bowls like Nell and Alice, they have two sets of tableware, one for everyday and one for special occasions. In the kitchen they have a breakfast bar and a machine that makes fizzy water.

Nell notices little bowls of dried leaves and flowers lying around the house, just like Grandma used to have, which make each room smell similar. When she leans in to smell the bowls they make her sneeze. The cottage smells of paint, or cooking, or the garden because Alice likes to leave the windows open.

Rachel and her parents don't have to wear jumpers inside because the house is always warm. In Rachel's house, the inside always feels like inside, whereas in

Nell's house the kitchen door is left open because of the turpentine fumes so the outside becomes part of the inside. She and Alice wear thick jumpers and two pairs of socks each.

Nell tells Rachel about the frog that once hopped into the kitchen.

'Ew,' Rachel,' says. 'That's gross. What if it jumped into your bed?'

Nell didn't mind the frog but she makes the same face as Rachel and agrees on the grossness.

Since starting school, Nell has come to understand that boys and girls are very different. In the playground, the girls huddle together and speak of secret things. They play with the long skipping-rope or make up games called Mummies and Babies. Nell invents a game about fairies that some of the others enjoy playing. The games she has made up herself are better as there is no confusion over the rules. She makes up another game about aliens on a new planet but it isn't liked as much.

The boys stay in a different part of the playground. They play football or run around bumping into each other. They look at worms under tree stumps.

Nell knows a boy would think it cool to have a frog in the kitchen. A boy would touch the frog then threaten his sister with his froggy fingers. A girl should not touch a frog. A girl should think a frog in the kitchen gross and scary. Nell wonders why Alice didn't explain these differences to her. She is determined to perfect this strange new art of being a girl.

Upstairs, Rachel explains that each bedroom has space-saving, fitted wardrobes and that Mrs Nunnally buys new duvets and pillows from Laura Ashley once a year because it's too much of a faff to take bedding to the dry-cleaners. Rachel explains all of this proudly, as if the Nunnallys have thought of a solution to everything. They have figured out the best way of living.

Going to Rachel's house after school becomes a regular occurrence. Mrs Nunnally tells Nell to call her *Jane* and that she can call Mr Nunnally *Alan*. In Nell's head Rachel's parents are still Mr and Mrs Nunnally. Other people's parents are like teachers; they do not have first names.

Late in November, they arrive home from school to find a dark-haired woman ironing in the kitchen. 'That's Magdeline,' Rachel says, as they take their toast through to the living room.

'But who is she?' Nell whispers.

'She's our cleaner. She does our washing and ironing. She hoovers and dusts and cleans the bathroom and kitchen. She tidies my room.' Rachel shows Nell the brown envelope kept behind the pink vase on the mantelpiece. 'This is where Mummy keeps the money for Magdeline. She pays her on a Friday.'

It occurs to Nell that her life with Alice is very different to life in Rachel's house. Alice would not want someone, a stranger, tidying things away so she wouldn't know where to find them. Nell peers into the brown envelope, at the crisp, flat notes. It seems to Nell to be an awful lot of money. She understands that she is not wealthy or, at least, that Alice would not have the money for such things as cleaners, whether she wanted one or not. The Nunnallys are the sort of people who fly on aeroplanes, eat in restaurants, and pay someone to do their ironing.

'Why doesn't your mum work?' Rachel asks.

Nell frowns. 'She's an artist.'

'I know,' Rachel says. 'But she could do that as a hobby. She could have a proper job as well.'

Nell isn't sure how to explain to Rachel that Alice's work is not a hobby. 'Sometimes she sells her paintings,' she tells Rachel. 'And she teaches drawing.'

'Can I come to your house?'

'I'll ask,' Nell says. 'Maybe you can come on Saturday.'

'Wow,' Rachel says, standing in Nell's kitchen. 'It's so crumbly.'

Nell likes this choice of word. She likes the way the curly c sounds on her tongue. The word reminds her of nice things: apple and blackberry crumble, digestive biscuits. Perhaps shabby, ramshackle (another word she likes) or messy, might be a better word to describe the kitchen: the green speckled tiles behind the sink, faded lino, pots of sprawling herbs, jam jars full of paint brushes and art books stacked precariously on top of cupboards, but Rachel uses crumbly and Nell loves her new friend even more for this.

From then on, Rachel often comes over to the cottage on Saturdays. It gives Mr and Mrs Nunnally time to themselves, Mr Nunnally says, winking at Alice when they drop Rachel off.

Nell and Rachel come rushing into the cottage kitchen one Saturday morning to find Alice holding a class. The kitchen table is in the garden so six people and their easels can be squashed into the tiny kitchen. In the middle of the room sits the model, a large-breasted woman with a mass of curly silver hair. Nell is used to this but Rachel stands open-mouthed.

'But why do the models have to be naked?' she asks Nell later. 'Why can't they wear swimming costumes?'

'It wouldn't be life drawing then,' Nell replies. 'Life drawing means naked drawing. They have to be naked.'

She thinks of the models sitting on the kitchen chair wearing swimming costumes or shorts, goggles hanging around their necks. The image is more absurd to Nell than their nakedness.

Just before Christmas there is a school trip planned. They have been doing science at school, learning about energy and electricity. Before electricity people had to use real fires, candles and gas lamps. You couldn't just turn a light on if you needed to get up in the night and go to the bathroom. Their teacher tells them about her great grandmother's younger sister who died because she didn't have a hairdryer. She was drying her hair close to the fire one evening and it caught alight. She was wearing a long white nightgown that buttoned all the way up to her chin. Her nightgown caught alight too. She couldn't pull if off, or put the fire out.

Nell would like to know more about this girl who died because she lived long ago and had no hairdryer. Didn't she have anything on hand to put out the fire with? Was no one there to help her? Did the room catch fire too? She wants to put her hand up and ask these questions but Mrs Reed has already moved on and is now explaining about coal irons and copper bed heaters.

The school trip is to a power station. Alice tells Nell she won't be able to go on the trip and Nell is cross. She wants to sit next to Rachel on the coach and share the earphones of Rachel's new portable CD player.

Alice and Nell are in the kitchen after dinner. Alice is drying the plates and Nell is putting the cutlery away in the drawer. She doesn't understand why the rest of the cottage can remain a mess, littered with paint palettes, art books and half-finished canvases, but the washing up must be done, dried and put away immediately after dinner.

'But why can't I go?'

'I did almost two months at Greenham Common. It's completely ridiculous to take children to a nuclear power station. You'll come home glowing. I'm going to write to your headteacher.'

'What's Greenham Common?' Nell asks.

'It was a peace camp,' Alice replies.

Nell frowns, thinking of a campsite full of peaceful people. Why does this mean she can't go on the school trip?

'But everyone else is going.'

Alice places a mug upside down on the kitchen counter, ready for Nell to dry and put away.

'I'll be the odd-one-out,' Nell tries again, shutting the cupboard a little harder than she intended.

'It's much better to be the odd-one-out than to be the same as everyone else.'

Nell sighs. She knows her classmates will notice her absence, and that she'll have to make something up. *Oh, I was sick that day*, she hears herself saying to the others in the playground. *It was so annoying.*

That night Nell dreams of a summer camp with tents, ball games and people with flowers in their hair clapping and singing happy songs. In the middle of the scene, a girl in a long white nightgown is screaming. Her hair is on fire but no one can see her.

13

2004

They are out for Teresa's birthday, all six of them: Teresa, Nell, Shirley, Molly, Becky, and Claire, the newly appointed assistant manager. They go to an Italian place in town. After they've split the bill and finished the last of the two bottles of wine on the table they walk up the High Street, intending to go for a drink in a bar called Tatters. The night is warm. It's mid July. Half a moon hangs in the sky above the clock tower as they make their way onto North Street. Brighton on a Friday night in summer is busy with not only students but groups of out-of-towners, down to enjoy the music scene, or else on stag or hen dos, romantic weekends. Couples walk hand in hand. Girls totter on high heels. A group of young men stagger into the road and are beeped at by a bus driver.

Nell has been living with Scott for almost a year. She doesn't go out much. There is always something she feels she should be doing in the flat. She has learned not to mention the girls from work when she's at home. Everyone, it seems, is a bad influence: someone she should not associate with for one reason or another. Teresa is not to be trusted because she must think Nell wants her job. Shirley is a busy-body, and Molly is a crazy hippy because she reads everyone their horoscopes in the morning and doesn't eat dairy.

They reach Tatters and head inside. The bar is very blue. Loud reggae music plays. Nell buys herself a glass of white wine. Her phone buzzes. She takes a sip of wine and moves towards the doors leading to the small outside area. 'I'll be back in a minute,' she calls to the others. She takes her phone from her pocket and opens Scott's text.

Need picking up? It's getting late.

We've just moved to Tatters.

Thought you were going for food.

Nell stares at Scott's reply, unsure of what to say. She did tell Scott they had a reservation at the restaurant. She hadn't known they'd be going to Tatters after. She hadn't known she might *want* to go. *We did*, she texts back. She pauses, staring at the screen. *I'm ready to leave if you're around to collect me.*

I'll see you in twenty minutes.

Nell takes a large gulp of wine, and then another. She heads inside. 'I'm really sorry. I've got to go.'

'What?' Becky says. 'We've only just got here.'

'Sorry.' Nell places her glass on the table.

She completes hasty goodbyes, smoothes her hair down then exits the bar. She'd rather be outside, waiting, just in case Scott is early. One day, last week, Nell still doesn't know why, Scott had come into the shop an hour before closing time. He'd wandered around for a while then told Nell he'd see her later.

'Was that your man?' Becky had asked.

Nell had given a slight nod, carried on stocking up the jewellery stand by the till.

Becky giggled. 'Thought you might have thrown your arms around him or something.'

'I'm sure she does at home,' Shirley had said.

'I'm sure she does more than that.'

Nell felt unable to look at either of them. 'Did we have another box of jewellery on the delivery or is this it?'

The temperature has dropped a degree or two. She puts her jacket on, then stands, clutching her bag, shifting from one foot to the other until she sees the Astra approaching.

Scott pulls up outside the bar. He's smoking a cigarette, his posture slightly hunched, one hand on the wheel. He leans over and opens the passenger door from the inside.

Nell climbs in. Scott watches her carefully as she shuts the door and reaches for her seatbelt. He's been drinking. Nell can see it in his eyes and smell it on his breath. He says nothing, only pulls away sharply. It isn't late but she imagines Scott will tell her she should have called him earlier. He'll say he needs his sleep because he has to get

114

up for work tomorrow. So does Nell, but all she does, according to Scott, is fart around tidying clothes all day. Silently, they make their way home, leaving Brighton, then Hove, behind. They have almost reached Shoreham and Nell thinks perhaps he will say nothing at all. They'll arrive home – Scott will toss his keys onto the coffee table. He'll have another beer, put the TV on, probably fall asleep. Sometimes he wakes up, turns the TV off, and comes to bed but more often than not, he doesn't. Nell prefers it that way, even though the noise of the TV often wakes her.

'You shouldn't go out like that.'

Scott's eyes haven't left the road but Nell looks down at what she is wearing; a denim skirt and white blouse. The skirt is just above her knee. She'd only bought the skirt and blouse last week. She thought Scott would like the blouse. He always approves if she wears a blouse.

'Like what?'

'Like that,' Scott says, glancing at her this time. 'That skirt. It isn't classy.' He flicks his cigarette out the window.

'I like it.' She'd noticed the skirt as soon as it came in and grabbed the size eight before Molly did.

They reach the roundabout and Scott's face darkens. 'It's slutty. If you're going to wear skirts, wear longer ones. You should try looking a little more elegant.'

Perhaps because of the wine, or perhaps because the evening is still warm and the streets are full of people out for the evening, Nell feels somehow safeguarded against Scott and his bad moods.

'I really like the skirt, Scott. It's just a skirt.'

Scott slams his hands on the steering wheel, causing Nell to jump and the car to swerve.

'Scott! Be careful!'

'You like it because you know everyone will be staring at you. Every guy in that place will have had an eyeful of your legs tonight. How do you think that makes me feel, huh? You think it's okay that I let my girlfriend prance about looking like a whore?'

'I wasn't prancing about. I—'

'All I want is to see you looking classy. All I want is for you to wear nice things and to see you looking like a woman.'

He's shouting now. The car swerves from one side of the road to the other. She realises he has been sitting at home drinking and stewing over the fact that she has gone out without him. His expression is fierce. He's got that look about him, both focused and glazed over at the same time. He's hunched over the wheel, driving way too fast.

'Please, Scott. Be careful.' Nell clings to the passenger door handle as Scott puts his foot down on the accelerator. 'There are cameras along here. You'll lose your licence.'

'And whose fault will that be?'

A car beeps because they are close to the middle of

the road. Scott pulls the Astra sharply back over and swears out the window.

'I'll throw the skirt away.'

Scott ignores her. He circles the skate park then stops the car and unfastens his seatbelt. Nell thinks they must be getting out so she unfastens hers too. Scott leans over her and opens the passenger door. Before she has time to react, he has pushed her, hard. She slams into the open car door and falls out onto the gravelly pavement. She is shocked but immediately sits up. Her palms are grazed and the left side of her body hurts. She touches her cheek and realises that her face is grazed too. She struggles to stand. She does not want Scott to see her looking so pathetic.

'Scott.'

He doesn't look at her. He leans across, slams the passenger door shut, starts the engine and drives away. She is sure he will circle around the skate park and come back for her. She waits. He doesn't.

Nell collects her handbag. She limps to the side of the curb to look for her shoe. For just a moment, she considers not going home, to Scott's flat. She could walk back towards Brighton, go to the house. Perhaps Robyn and Kelly-Ann are still there. Perhaps they will let her stay the night. She will tell them what happened and they will convince her not to go home. Cups of milky tea will be brought to her, the sofa bed made. But what if they have both moved out by now? Or what if they look at her in confusion and say, 'Nell, why are you here? You don't live here anymore.'

What if Robyn says, 'I told you so.'

Nell thinks she probably has enough in her bank account to allow her to stay the night in a hotel in town, or the hostel. She will sneak back to the flat tomorrow and collect her things. But then what will she do? She shivers on the pavement. Scott is expecting her to walk home. If she isn't back soon he is likely to come looking for her. She crosses the road and limps along the pavement.

14

In the morning, when Scott notices Nell applying extra make-up, trying to cover the graze on her face, he says, 'I told you, you can't handle your booze. You're too small. There's nothing to soak up the alcohol.'

Nell's eyes shift slowly to Scott, behind her, in the wardrobe mirror.

'You couldn't even stand up straight.' He goes into the hallway. 'I'm leaving in five minutes, if you want a lift.'

Nell stares at her reflection. *Was I so drunk I couldn't stand up straight? Did I fall out of the car?*

She tells the girls at work that she slipped on the steps to the entrance of the flats when she got home.

'You might scar,' Molly says, frowning at Nell's face. 'You'll have to get some Bio-Oil.'

Scott doesn't mention the incident again and, before long, the bruise on Nell's shoulder has faded, the graze on her knee healed, the scratch on her face almost gone. Whether she fell or whether she provoked Scott to the point of pushing her no longer seems to matter. Scott would never intentionally hurt her. Just because Nell never gets angry, never loses her temper, it doesn't mean that it isn't perfectly normal to do so.

It is she who is abnormal, she who is cold, unfeeling, unemotional.

She thinks this when Scott, angry one evening because she bought the the wrong type of beer from the supermarket, throws a can at her, narrowly missing her head. No harm done. Just a mark on the wall that can be painted over. If she could only be the kind of girlfriend Scott needs and deserves, everything would be fine and he wouldn't get so angry.

She tells herself this when, after answering the door to the postman early one morning in her dressing gown, and chatting to him about the weather whilst signing for Scott's new trainers, Scott grabs her arm in the kitchen and twists it behind her back. 'What were you talking to that greasy little prick about? Is this what you do when I'm not here, huh? Open the door half naked and show the postman your tits?'

'I-I'm sorry,' Nell had said, her eyes filling up with tears from the pain in her shoulder. She shouldn't have opened the door like that. She shouldn't be so careless.

He had let go of her arm but she'd had pain in her shoulder for several days.

When Scott hits her one evening, Nell is so unsurprised she calmly goes to the bathroom and applies a cold flannel to her eye. *You idiot*, she tells the reflection that stares back at her. *Why did you have to say that? Why couldn't you have kept quiet?*

Scott had been watching a quiz show.

'My team always wins the Friday pub quiz,' a woman in a red sparkly jumper had told the host.

Nell was in the kitchen drying the plates and saucepans she'd used for dinner, only half listening to the TV. Scott was on the sofa.

'Which fifteenth-century Italian painter is famous for *The Beheading of Saint John the Baptist*?' the host asked.

'Must be that bloke who did that woman with the funny fucking grin,' Scott had said, sipping his beer. 'What was his name? De Vinci. Leonardo. That's it.' Scott had glanced at Nell who had said nothing. The woman on the screen was frowning. 'I should know this one. We went to Florence for my sixtieth.'

'No, wait,' Scott had said. 'It's Michael Fucking Angelo. Must be.' He'd shot Nell a sideways glance, expecting her to agree.

'Now you're just naming Ninja Turtles,' she had said, smiling and reaching to put a plate in the cupboard. 'And you're about a hundred years too early.'

Scott calmly stood up from the sofa, walked into the kitchen and punched her in the face.

Nell had fallen backwards against the sink, to the floor. She didn't have time to register the pain before Scott grabbed the neck of her jumper and hauled her to her feet.

'Who the fuck is it then?' he'd hissed at her, his spit spraying her face.

'C-Caravaggio,' she'd stammered, her voice hoarse. 'It's Caravaggio.'

Scott, not quite through with her, shoved her against the sink and walked away, back to the TV, muttering to himself. Nell leant against the kitchen counter blinking rapidly, her face throbbing. She managed to get from the kitchen to the bathroom where she'd run a flannel under the cold tap then slumped to the floor. She'd sat like that for some time, leaning against the bath, the cold flannel pressed against her eye. There was something wrong with her life and yet she had no idea how to change it. She thought of herself arriving in Brighton, finding her room, living in the house with Kelly-Ann and Robyn. That person was someone different.

But Scott loved her. He had wanted her to live with him, for them to share their lives. She had made him feel stupid. If she didn't know anything about fifteenth-century Italian painters, she would never have embarrassed Scott and he wouldn't have been angry. Her sheltered upbringing has made her stuck-up and ungrateful, just like Scott says.

The next day at work, she tells the others she walked into one of the kitchen cupboards. 'The corner of it caught me.' No one questioned her. Only Shirley frowned and

122

looked, for just a moment, at Nell in a way that indicated she wasn't entirely convinced by her story.

Scott had said very little after Nell had picked herself up from the bathroom floor and returned to the kitchen to finish putting the dishes away. The following morning, though, he had glanced at her eye and said, 'I don't know, Nell. My older sister was much cleverer than me. She was always telling me how stupid I was, laughing at me. I saw red, you know. It wasn't you.'

'Let's just forget it.'

Scott had then gone into the kitchen and returned with tea and toast. 'I've made you breakfast.'

After the quiz show incident Nell did her best to minimise the potential threat that was Scott's anger and disgust with her. She watched herself carefully, never challenging him. She never bought anything without consulting him first. She tried to cook the food he preferred, wore what she knew he would think appropriate. She had sex whenever Scott wanted sex, despite the way the sex made her feel: worthless, and that she was giving a part of herself away. All this was a small price to pay for Scott's calmer moods.

The supervisor position came up at work and this time Nell took it. Becky had told her, before she'd told Teresa, that she was leaving, taking a job as a teaching assistant in a primary school. They'd been in the stockroom last Wednesday morning unpacking and checking off the delivery. 'They say if I do it for a year or two and the school likes me, I might be able to go on a training scheme.'

'That's brilliant. I'm so pleased for you, Becky.'

'I've got to do something else,' Becky said, pulling a handful of scarves out of the tote box. 'I can't be here forever.'

'I know,' Nell had said.

'But what about you, Nell?'

She'd shrugged. 'I'm fine, Becky. I like it here.'

Becky shook her head. 'If anyone should be doing something else, Nell, it's you. Remember when we had that line in, the dresses with the lace and the fringe, those pleated skirts and the headbands with the feathers. What was it called, Daisy something?'

'Buchanan.'

'You knew immediately why it was called that, that it was because of *The Great Gatsby* which meant the clothes were from the twenties. You know, that style. You know so many things. All those books you read…You should be doing something else. You could do *anything*.'

Nell had reached for the pliers to cut the cable tie on the next box. 'I don't know.'

'Promise me you'll at least think about it?'

'I'll think about it.'

Becky reached into the tote and pulled out a handful of reduced cardigans in strange colours: a yellow that was too limey, a purple that was too brown, a traffic-light orange. The buttons on the cardigans were star-shaped. 'Why are they sending us this crap?' Becky said. 'This is from two seasons ago. We've sent it back once already.'

'It's to bulk out our sale area.'

'Thank God I won't be here for the sale.' She turned to Nell, waving the cardigans as she spoke. 'At least take the bloody supervisor position in the meantime. Teresa will kill you if you don't. She can't stand interviewing.' Becky reached for the clipboard. 'Jesus, these cardigans are seventy per cent off. They can't give them away.'

The following week Teresa had invited Nell into the office for a chat. 'We'll have to advertise for a few weeks. I might have to do a couple of interviews. I'll have to interview you too, so the paperwork can go in your file but, Nell, you'd be crazy not to take it. You do the job already.'

And so Nell had taken the position, which had pleased Scott. 'See. I knew you'd go far in that company. We should celebrate. I'll take you out for dinner. Let's go to that Italian you like.'

Nell felt relieved Scott was happy about her promotion. The bruise under her eye healed and several weeks passed in which she hadn't angered Scott. He even suggested they take a holiday together in the summer. 'Spain,' he said. 'We'll go to Spain. Get some travel brochures on your lunch break.'

15

1997

Towards the end of Year Six Nell's body begins to change. She develops small breasts and notices hairs between her legs. She feels a mix of fear and amazement. The additions to her self are scary, and seem to happen quickly, yet she marvels at the fact her body can change in such a way without her instruction. Once she gets used to them, these changes, although strange, make her feel pleased. She has always looked forward to growing up. Already she thinks about leaving home. She sees herself living in an apartment in New York, part Rachel, part Phoebe, and with a dash of Monica. She'll have a great job. She'll take the subway and ride in yellow taxis. She'll go on dates and fall in love and sit around with her friends drinking coffee. Nell has no doubt that this is exactly how life will be. Secondary school will be just like the *Sweet Valley High* books she borrows from the library, and her twenties will be like *Friends*.

'One day I will go to America,' she tells Alice, being careful not to mention her father in case this upsets her.

'You'd better start saving then.'

Nell empties her old sweet tin, the one Grandma kept her parking change in, and sits on her bed counting her coins. Eight pounds will not get her to America. It probably won't even get her to Grimsby. She feels sure, though, that she will have enough money for America by the time she is ready to go.

After school one afternoon, Rachel suggests they practise kissing. Nell isn't sure why but the practice of kissing requires they wear lipstick. Rachel has a make-up box, given to her by her Aunt Caroline who works in Debenhams. The box is full of samples, little packets of face cream, mini mascara and broken lipsticks. Nell has only seen Rachel's Aunt Caroline in the wedding photograph Rachel keeps on the windowsill next to her ballerina jewellery box and collection of pottery animals. Aunt Caroline has red lips and thin eyebrows. She wears a long, white wedding dress that has squashed her breasts upwards into two large mounds.

Rachel had been Aunt Caroline's bridesmaid. This meant she got to wear a red satin dress and carry white roses. Rachel has been a bridesmaid twice, last summer for her Aunt Caroline and two years ago for her Aunt Vanessa. She was given jewellery on both occasions and got to keep the dresses. Nell knows she will never be a bridesmaid because to be a bridesmaid you appear to need aunts who are not yet married and Nell does not have any aunts, married or not.

Nell and Rachel sit on Rachel's bed with the box of make-up. They apply the lipstick, taking turns to use the compact mirror then pressing their lips onto a tissue, creating two red half-moons. This is the way Mrs Nunnally applies her lipstick and therefore this must be the correct thing to do.

Rachel tells Nell that they have to stand in front of her full-length mirror.

'Kiss the mirror and imagine it's a boy,' Rachel tells her. 'I'll show you.' She leans in, placing her lips on the glass. 'Mmmmm.'

Nell looks away. She isn't sure she wants to watch Rachel kissing a mirror.

'Now it's your turn,' Rachel tells her, returning to the bed.

Nell walks over to the mirror. She stares at her reflection. Her thick curly hair falls over her left eye. The lipstick makes her look like someone people would notice. She does not want to be noticed.

'Go on,' Rachel says. 'We've got to practise.'

Nell closes her eyes. She leans in and presses her lips against the glass. She tries to think of the boys she knows but the thought of kissing any of the boys from school is disgusting. Instead she thinks only of kissing a mirror.

She pulls away and stares at the smudge of lipstick next to Rachel's smudge.

'That's good,' Rachel says. 'Now we'll both be ready for when a boy kisses us.'

It's the summer holidays. In three weeks' time Nell will start school again but this time it will be a different, bigger school.

Rachel and Nell are on the swings in Rachel's back garden sucking sherbet lemons. They can hear the hum of a neighbour's lawnmower. A skylark circles above them, spinning its song. It's a hot day, the air is muggy, with little breeze.

They are both wearing shorts. Rachel's are sporty and have stripes at the sides whilst Nell's are faded denim. Rachel wears a yellow top with a rainbow on the front and Nell wears her favourite soft, blue T-shirt. Really, they are too big for the swings now. Their legs are too long and the frame groans as they swing, their thighs sticking to the faded and cracked yellow plastic seats. They like to peel large chunks of paint from the rusting metal fame. At their feet is Rachel's cat, Mustard, in a travelling basket. Mustard is not happy. His green eyes stare accusingly at them from behind the grill.

Rachel will not be coming to Nell's new school because Rachel is moving away. Two large removal lorries are parked at the front of the house. Burly men are securing the last of the furniture with ropes whilst Rachel's parents fill the car with their essential items: a kettle and three enamel mugs, toothbrushes and toothpaste, bleach spray, food for Mustard and a chilli plant. Nell, when she'd arrived, had noticed all of these items on top of four large bags in the hallway labelled *Car*.

Rachel is not needed until they are ready to leave. Her bedroom, her furniture, and all her things have been sorted and packed into one of the large lorries. Rachel must stay out of the way and not get under anyone's feet.

Nell has come to watch, and to say goodbye.

The swings are in the shady part of the garden, next to the apple trees. The dappled sunlight falls across Nell's thighs as she pushes the toes of her trainers against the dry lawn and sucks on her sweet. It cracks and she can taste its sherbety centre fizzing on her tongue. She looks at the fluffy hairs on her legs and wonders if she should start shaving.

Although Nell knows that Rachel is moving, she cannot fully grasp that it is happening, that today is the day.

Rachel had told her, several weeks ago, before they broke up from school. They'd gone to their bags to collect their break snacks: a banana for Nell and a Tracker bar for Rachel, then sat on the bench next to the tree that was planted for a girl who had attended the school and who had died suddenly of a heart condition. No one in their class knew the girl because she had died four years ago but everyone knew her name because of the plaque on the bench next to the tree. *In Loving Memory of Sarah Jane Peters, 1982–1993.*

Nell often thinks about Sarah Jane Peters. She wonders what she had looked like, what her favourite lessons had been and if she liked animals. Sarah Jane Peters must have sat in the hall and eaten her lunch from the same grey lunch trays as Nell does. She must have practised long jump on the school field. Probably, she'd plaited her friends' hair at break time and collected conkers on the way home from school, just like Nell and Rachel. Sarah Jane Peters dying was wrong and out of order. The fact that such things can happen makes Nell feel anxious.

'I've got something to tell you,' Rachel had said.

Nell had known immediately that this would not be a good something.

'My dad's got a new job. My mum says we'll have more money for holidays and my dad says I can have a horse.' Rachel plucked at a loose thread hanging from her school dress. 'The thing is, we're moving to Devon which is far away.'

On the school map of the British Isles that hangs on their classroom wall, Devon is right down at the bottom of the country, in the bit that sticks out like a foot. Devon is not anywhere near Lincolnshire.

'You know I've always wanted a horse. We can write

to each other,' Rachel said, 'like pen-friends. And when Alice gets a computer you can get an email address, like me, and we can email.'

Rachel's parents bought her a brand-new computer last year: there's a funny box that makes a screeching noise when it's connecting to the World Wide Web. Alice would not want a computer in the cottage. It would take up too much space, she wouldn't like the screeching noise and it would probably cause cancer.

'I can email you from school,' Nell said quietly. 'Or the library.'

'We can still be best friends.'

She could tell from Rachel's voice that Rachel was unsure as to whether this would really be the case. From what Nell knows about best friends they are supposed to see each other every day, or at least most days. They share secrets and tell each other about their dreams. This will be hard to do with one person at the bottom of the country and the other person nearer to the middle.

Nell had watched three younger girls doing cartwheels on the school playing field. She has never been able to cartwheel and always feels envious of the girls who throw themselves at the grass, legs in the air, blue gingham dresses falling to reveal dazzling white knickers. For just a second they are a perfect star. She wants to be that perfect star.

Nell watched Rachel eating her Tracker bar. Rachel

moving away would work out fine for Rachel but not for her. She didn't tell Rachel because this would not be Rachel's problem. This unexpected turn of events required her to be brave. 'I'm glad about your horse,' she'd said.

Now here they are sitting on the swings with Mustard at their feet. Nell wonders who will be moving into Rachel's house once they have gone. The thought of someone else living there is strange. The house belongs to Rachel and her family. Never again will Mr Nunnally come home from work late, place his bag in the hallway and wash his hands in the downstairs loo with the honey-scented soap before dinner. Mrs Nunnally will no longer listen to Radio One, or her Boyzone CD, whilst unloading the dishwasher.

Mrs Nunnally is calling Rachel. She appears at the garden gate with the small envelope of keys they must drop in to the estate agents on the way.

'Rachel, we're leaving now.'

'I have to go,' Rachel says, sliding off the swing and lifting Mustard.

Mrs Nunnally smiles when she sees Nell. 'I can't wait for you to come and visit us in our new home, Nell.'

'Me too.' Nell prods a daisy with the toe of her trainer. She doesn't know how to get to Devon.

At the front of the house, the removal lorries have already left and the front door is closed for the last time.

'I'll call you when we arrive,' Rachel says, her eyes wet with tears. She gets into the back of the car with Mustard and secures his carry case with a seatbelt.

Nell watches as Mr Nunnally starts the engine and Mrs Nunnally leans forward to fiddle with the radio. Rachel is waving. Nell tries to make her wave as enthusiastic as Rachel's but fails. Her wave is heavy and fake and she feels like a bad person for wishing that Rachel's dad did not have the opportunity to earn more money putting his hands up cows' bottoms and putting hamsters down in Devon rather then Lincolnshire. She wishes, just for a moment, that Rachel's mum didn't want more holidays and that Rachel could be frightened of horses.

As the car makes its way along the street for the last time, Nell has a sick feeling in her stomach. She wonders if she has eaten too many sherbet lemons.

Nell received her first letter from Rachel three weeks after she'd moved. Three weeks had seemed a very long time. She'd checked the doormat every morning, sometimes looking underneath it, or else running outside and making sure the postman hadn't accidentally dropped a letter on the path, not that she had ever found a letter on the path before.

Rachel has met a girl called Holly at the stables who has a horse called Velvet. Holly will allow Nell to ride Velvet when Nell comes to visit. *She doesn't usually let*

134

people ride him but I told Holly you are my best friend.
Rachel goes on to tell Nell more about Holly. She has
three girl gerbils: Suki, Matilda and Prudence. They like
to chew bits of wood and sleep on each other's heads.
Holly has a Labrador puppy called Simon and a karaoke
machine which she got for her birthday. Rachel writes a
lot about Holly, about how they will both be starting at
the same school next month and how they have arranged
to meet at the post box to walk in together. Rachel stayed
over at Holly's house last weekend. They sang *Wannabe*
on Holly's karaoke machine. Rachel dressed up as Sporty
Spice and Holly was Baby Spice. They ate chocolate ice
cream and watched *Dawson's Creek.*

Nell had frowned and put the letter down on the
kitchen table. She had imagined Rachel sitting in her
bedroom surrounded by unpacked boxes, gazing out of
the window and feeling sad to be away from her best
friend when in fact she was at Holly's house feeding
gerbils, watching *Dawson's Creek* and singing *Wannabe.*
She feels as though she is being replaced, like the
Nunnallys' duvets. 'Out with the old and in with the
new,' Mrs Nunnally used to say.

16

2005

It's a dim January afternoon. Scott and Nell are sitting in the pub waiting for Alice. Nell hasn't seen Alice for over two years. Scott chose the pub, somewhere on the edge of Peterborough, not far from the motorway and accessible to everyone. Alice had said she'd be there at two. The meeting had been Scott's idea. 'I can't believe you haven't seen your own mother for two years. We should meet up.' Nell had been reluctant but, once Scott gets an idea into his head, it's impossible to try to dissuade him. Not wanting to create tension, she had agreed. She couldn't work out why Scott wanted to meet Alice anyway, seeing as everything he said about her was negative. Nell had reminded him she had never met *his* parents, but he had brushed her remark aside, telling her it was different because his parents had each other and his sister, whereas Alice didn't have anyone. He was thoughtful like that.

Nell had rung Alice and Alice had said, 'Of course. How lovely.' She had expected Alice to be surprised, but nothing ever surprised Alice. She'd taken down the address of the pub along with the date, a week on Thursday – Nell's day off – and told her that she was looking forward to seeing them both.

'Well that's that,' Scott had said, satisfied. 'I get to meet the famous artist.'

Nell had stared at her phone, feeling uneasy.

They arrive early. 'So we can get a pint in,' Scott says, but Nell doesn't feel like drinking.

The pub is full of brown and wasted afternoons. The dark wood, swirly carpets and heavy curtains that probably existed before the smoking ban give the pub an out-of-time feel. This is a pub that should have been bulldozed several years ago to make way for new flats, or a Holiday Inn.

The woman behind the bar jabs her thumb in the direction of the dining room. 'You can take your drinks through there if you're having the carvery.'

The dining room smells of boiled cabbage and vinegar. A teenage boy stands behind the counter looking at his phone; an elderly couple in the corner are eating silently. Nell and Scott take their drinks over to a table by the window with a view of the car park.

Nell can't quite believe it's been two years since she last saw Alice – she has been living with Scott for eighteen months. She sips her apple juice, keeping an eye on the door. She drums her fingers on the table, smooths down her hair.

'I don't know why you're so jittery. She's your mother.'

I don't want to be here. I don't want to be here.

The words flash in her mind, a neon red warning. The feeling is a familiar one. It isn't that she doesn't want to see Alice, more the feeling of desperately needing to escape. Lately, she's felt more and more like she's standing still while the ground moves beneath her feet, pulling her, against her will, in a direction she doesn't want to go.

Nell puts her hands in her lap, trying to keep them still. She takes a deep, steadying breath. Alice appears in the doorway. She's wearing a slim-fitting pair of jeans and a long black cardigan. Moving towards Alice, Nell notices the silver hooped earrings Alice saves for special occasions, along with mascara. Alice has made a special effort and, for some reason, this makes Nell feel guilty. They hug, briefly, whilst Scott watches.

'This is Scott.' Nell pulls away from Alice.

Alice and Scott shake hands and Scott gives Alice his dimpled smile. 'It's great to finally meet you,' he says. 'I've heard so much about you.'

Alice drapes her coat over the spare chair. 'I haven't heard much about you.'

Nell winces but Scott smiles. 'Shall we get some grub then? I don't know about you, ladies, but I'm starving.'

They go to the carvery where Scott piles his plate with food. Alice has a few slices of chicken and vegetables. Nell has the same but adds potatoes and a Yorkshire pudding so that Scott won't be cross with her. 'I pay for you to eat and you don't eat,' she can imagine him saying later in the car.

Chairs are pulled in, paper napkins unfolded. 'So, how was the exhibition in Manchester?' Nell asks, remembering Alice's last email.

'Good. The gallery are happy. I sold four paintings.'

'So the painting's going well then?' Scott says, with an amused expression.

Alice watches Scott fold a large slice of beef into his mouth. 'It's going well,' she says.

Nell tries to eat but the meat is dry, the vegetables overcooked. She drinks all of her apple juice in an attempt to make the food go down more easily. She scratches her hand under the table until she notices Alice looking at her.

Scott glances at Nell's plate. 'I'm always telling her she should eat more.' He shoves his fork into a mound of cabbage. 'I keep telling her it isn't healthy to be so skinny.'

Alice swallows and takes a sip of water. She looks as though she is about to say something but changes her mind. Instead she asks Nell what she's been reading. The question depresses Nell although she isn't sure why.

'You know,' Scott says, interrupting, 'apart from all of that Biff, Chip and Kipper stuff we did at school, I've never read a story book in my life. I like to read the paper. And I sometimes read books about businessmen, you know people that have made it in life. *Really* made it.'

Alice looks from Nell to Scott and Nell is annoyed because she can see Alice is judging Scott. She finds herself silently defending him. *Not everyone has to know about art and literature. Not everyone has to be like you.* She reaches for her apple juice, then realises there is nothing left in the glass.

'Well everything is fine at home,' Alice says, breaking the silence. 'I've had a clear out, and I've painted the shed.'

Nell experiences a pang of homesickness as she thinks of the cottage. She pictures the view from the back door: a huge purple sky, the sun lowering into the hedgerows. She can hear the coo of a dove and jazz music playing from Alice's old radio. She remembers the smell of the garden after rain, and the lingering, ever present smell of oil paints and turpentine. She can see Alice's brushes drying on the draining board, a stew simmering on the hob. She swallows hard and pushes her knife and fork together on her plate. *All of that has gone*, she reminds herself. *All of that is lost.* She looks at Scott. *I am an adult and this is my life now.* Who is she angry with? With Scott for insisting on this stupid lunch? With Alice for being so polite when it is clear she has plenty of opinions about Nell's life? With her teachers for not trying harder to persuade her to stay on at school? With herself for fucking her life up so spectacularly?

'That was great,' Scott says, pushing his plate to one side. He wipes his hand on his tracksuit trousers.

Alice doesn't comment. It's clear she doesn't agree, or that her thoughts are elsewhere. She has left half her food. 'Do we pay at the bar, or do they come over?'

'I think we go to the bar,' Nell says quietly.

They stand, pushing the chairs back across the worn carpet. At the bar, Scott insists on paying. Alice raises an eyebrow as he produces a wad of cash from his wallet.

It's windy and Nell zips up her coat. Alice pulls her cardigan around her. Grandma's purple car is parked a few spaces away from Scott's Astra.

'Well,' Alice says. 'I'd better be going, before the traffic gets bad.'

'Sure,' Scott says. 'It was lovely to meet you, Alice.'

Alice studies Scott's face, as if looking for something, some clue that will help her figure out what he is doing with her daughter. Nell sees this look and feels both irritated and a sense of despair. Whatever Alice is looking for she is clearly unable to find it.

Alice's embrace is brief but, just for a moment, she squeezes Nell tightly against her. Then she is going, climbing into her car.

'Come on,' Scott says.

On the way home, Nell stares out of the window at the slow-moving motorway traffic. Scott switches the radio on. Two men are talking about a football match.

'That went well,' Scott says, smugly. 'Although I don't think she thought much of the food, probably used to finer cuisine, her being a famous artist and all that.'

Nell leans back in her seat and watches the passing landscape; the smudged green verges sandwiched between grey road and grey sky. She closes her eyes and pretends to sleep.

On Tuesday afternoon, Nell is in the stockroom filling a rail with sale dresses when her phone buzzes in her pocket. If she had been on the shop floor she wouldn't have been able to take the call. She looks at the screen. It's Alice, calling from the cottage.

'Hello.'

'He's an arsehole,' Alice says.

Nell feels a tightening in her chest. She sits down on the kick stool.

'I just can't work it out,' Alice is saying. 'When you said you had a boyfriend in Brighton, that you'd moved in together, I don't know, I imagined a nice boy. A vegan perhaps. Someone who plays the guitar. I mean, how *old* is he?'

Nell grips the phone. 'He's thirty-three,' she says.

Alice sighs. 'Anyway, It isn't about that. *Age.* It's about him. He's clearly an idiot, but there's something else, something creepy, about him.'

'There's nothing wrong with Scott. Just because he doesn't play the *guitar*—'

'Oh, come on, Nell. I wouldn't care if he was a bloody accountant, as long as he was nice, as long as you were happy. But you're not. You're more miserable than you were when you left. I hoped you would find friends that made you happy. That man is sucking the life out of you.'

'If you don't like him that's fine because you never have to see him again, or me,' she adds.

Alice is silent for a moment. 'Come home.'

Nell can hear the door that leads from the shop to the back area swinging open. She hangs up.

March. Almost three months since Nell last spoke to Alice. She's making toast in the kitchen when she receives a text from Teresa. *Can't get in. Been throwing up all night. Seafood. Not pregnant!* It's Claire's day off so Nell will be running the shop on her own.

Scott drops Nell at work for eight thirty. It's just Nell and Shirley until Molly gets in.

When Molly arrives to start her eleven o'clock shift, she looks awful – pale and sweaty.

After spending an hour on the shop floor, she wobbles over to Nell and leans feebly against the till point. 'I'm sorry, Nell. I thought I'd be okay. I'm going to have to go. It's just period pain but I can hardly stand.'

'Will you be able to get home?'

'I think I'll have to treat myself to a taxi.'

Once Molly has left, Nell realises that leaves only Becky on the late shift. Nell is on the early, due to leave at five thirty. She'll have to stay until eight with Becky now. It's too late to organise anything else. In the office, she looks inside her bag. She is unable to find her phone. She must have left it in the kitchen this morning after texting Teresa back. She logs onto the office PC and sends Scott a quick email, explaining what has happened and that she won't be home until late. Then she uses the internet to find the telephone number that will get her through to Scott's office.

'Hello, Anthony speaking.'

There is such a high turnover of staff, Nell can never remember who is who.

'Hi Anthony, is Scott there, please?'

'Who's calling?'

'It's Nell.'

'He's interviewing at the moment. I can take a message if you like.'

'Could you tell him I've got to work until eight tonight, please.'

'Sure,' Anthony says. 'No problem at all.'

* * *

When Nell arrives at the flat, it's after nine. She feels tired and hungry and can't wait to get in and make tea and toast before bed. The hallway is dark and she can hear the sound of the TV coming from the living room. She removes her shoes, rubs her feet, then hangs her jacket on the peg rail, not bothering to turn the light on. The lights in the living room and kitchen are also all off. The TV bathes the flat in an eerie blue glow.

'Scott?'

She hears footsteps behind her. A sharp shove. She is pushed forward. She falls against the coffee table, banging her shin and scattering beer cans onto the carpet.

'Where the fuck have you been.' Scott grabs her wrist, twisting it so hard she yelps. He pulls her to her feet.

'Scott, please.' Her voice sounds pathetic and she hates herself for not being able to get her words out quickly enough, to explain why she is home late.

'Who have you been out with?'

'No one. I—'

'I've been calling your phone for fucking hours!' He still has hold of her wrist.

'Please. I'm sorry, I left it here. It's probably on silent.'

'I'm tired of your excuses.'

'Molly was sick. I had to stay late. I called your office but—'

'You're full of bullshit, you know that? You think I deserve to put up with this?'

'I don't think—'

'I wasn't asking for your fucking opinion!' Scott releases her wrist.

Nell opens her mouth, trying once again to explain again about the sickness at work, about her call to Anthony, and how he must not have passed her message on, but before she can say anything more, Scott swings a fist towards her.

When she wakes, it is morning and Scott is standing over her, dressed for work. Nell jumps and scrambles to get up. Scott takes a step back, as if it is Nell who has frightened him.

'You'll be late for work,' he says. 'If you don't hurry up.' He stares at Nell, at her half-closed, swollen eye, as if she is something alien, something he can't figure out.

Nell swallows. 'I'll take a sick day,' she whispers.

'Suit yourself.'

She waits several minutes after hearing the front door close before getting off the sofa. In the bathroom she splashes cold water on her eye. She has a nasty bruise, worse than the one before, and a small cut above her eye. She takes a shower then dresses as best she can. Her wrist hurts and she tries to gently flex it. It isn't broken, probably just sprained.

She finds the roll of bandage in the kitchen drawer behind a box of plasters and an ancient pot of tiger balm, then wraps the bandage tightly around her wrist. In the bedroom, she pauses, catching sight of herself in the wardrobe mirror. She touches her reflection with her fingertips. *Is that you?* There is something about her that is no longer whole. She is an outline, like the kind Alice would make when beginning a drawing. Perhaps she was once fully there but has faded, or been rubbed out.

She opens the wardrobe and takes her rucksack from the bottom shelf where it sits next to two of Scott's old prosthetic legs. They look strange, lined up together like a pair, only not a pair. She begins to pack, taking very little: jeans, a jumper she is fond of, her laptop, a few toiletries, her purse.

In the kitchen, she finds her phone and discovers the thirty-six missed calls along with eleven text messages that Scott sent last night.

There is no answer from Teresa's phone so she leaves a message explaining that she won't be in, not only today, but ever. She apologises for the problem this will cause. She understands that leaving without notice means she will never be able to be re-employed by the company. She thanks Teresa for all she has done for her. After she has finished leaving the message, Nell zips her phone into the front compartment of her rucksack then quickly changes her mind, taking it out and leaving it on the kitchen counter. Her trainers on, she grabs her coat from the peg rail and leaves the flat, walking quickly down the stairwell to the front entrance, then out into the weak March sunshine. She takes her sunglasses from her rucksack – she wants to hide her swollen eye – and walks in the direction of the bus stop.

Part Three

17

1997

Autumn. The field behind the cottage has been harvested, the earth churned into long channels of mud. Other fields nearby are full of sugar beet, winter barley and leeks. The cows have all been brought inside. Nell sits at the kitchen table with a bowl of porridge. She can hear Alice moving around upstairs. The coffee in the French press next to the kettle is still warm.

She stirs her porridge with a teaspoon and listens to the creaking of the floorboards above her. The mornings are cold and she sits at the table in her uniform and coat. She reads the back of the box, about the rolled oats from Scotland, whilst pushing the thick gloopy mixture around in her bowl until the honey disappears.

Nell's secondary school is a long, flat, nineteen sixties building that she always thinks looks, from a distance, more like a factory than a school: a factory that does not make girls and boys exactly, rather holds them until they are ready for unleashing. The classrooms are cold, the windows often dirty. In each classroom there are grey tables and rows of brown plastic chairs. Her lessons are punctuated by the ringing of the bells and the slamming of lockers. The lower school pupils rush through the corridors like shoals of flapping fish. The shiny, green-tinged corridor floors have a clinical feel. There are black scuff marks along the bottoms of the walls. The older girls stand at their lockers in their rolled skirts applying make-up. The rule is not to look at the older girls when you pass them. You are of no consequence to them. They know about things that you do not.

In the classrooms they have to sit boy, girl, boy, girl. This is because a boy and a girl are less likely to talk to each other. Nell often sits next to Robbie Lock because there are no other M's in her tutor group.

Nell is more aware of the boys in secondary school. They have become different, other, or perhaps they have always been different, but it is only now that their differences have become noticeable. The boys smell of earth, unwashed skin, flaky scalps and cheap deodorant. Their uniforms are shabbier than the girls' uniforms. They wear their ties loose around their necks until they are told to tie them properly. They don't care if their shirts are creased or if they have scorch marks on their blazers from cigarette lighters or Bunsen burners. It doesn't matter if they have holes in their socks, in fact it seems better if they do.

A girl must not have holes or ladders in her tights

but, if a hole or ladder is acquired throughout the course of the day, a girl must not change into a new pair. She must sigh dramatically then sit down and slowly apply clear nail varnish as though she is dressing a wound. She must wear her hole or ladder with pride whilst constantly reminding the others how annoying it is. Girls must have interesting pencil cases, either their favourite boy band or something they can doodle stars on. They must have coloured gel pens, rubbers in the shape of hearts and a highlighter pen, but not yellow because yellow is boring and ordinary and is what the teachers use. Boys don't have to worry about having the right pencil case with the right things inside it, or even having a pencil case at all. It doesn't matter if they don't have a compass or a pencil sharpener or if their ink cartridges leak. They will borrow a compass or pencil sharpener from the girl they are sitting next to because girls always have these things.

The boys respect the girls with big breasts. They are a little in awe of these girls and they give them plenty of room in the corridors.

Girls smell of fruit shampoo, pressed powder, hair mousse, cherry lip balm, mint chewing gum and body spray with names like *Mysterious Musk* and *Temptation*. At least the popular girls do. The non-popular girls smell of anti-dandruff shampoo and stale sweat.

Nell is one of the popular girls. She is pleased about this. And why shouldn't she be? She is clever. Pretty, she thinks, in a petite and mousey sort of way. She doesn't have big breasts, but she doesn't suffer from acne. She can hide her eczema under her shirt. She knows about the TV programmes and films the girls at school like because she used to watch them with Rachel. She can quote from *Clueless* and she always listens to the top forty on a Sunday evening. She is not like Amanda Drew who smells, wears trousers that are too short for her and doesn't even bother with concealer to cover her spots.

At home, Alice's once comforting presence has begun to irritate Nell. It is as if the cottage is growing smaller whilst she is growing bigger. Alice is somehow always *there*. Nell wishes Alice would get a proper job so she could be out most of the time like other, normal, parents. At night Nell can hear Alice through the wall, coughing or moving restlessly around her room.

In the mornings, as soon as Nell wakes, she puts the radio on. She needs something to connect her to the outside world, something that isn't just Alice, the cottage, the fields, the cawing crows or the sound of the tractor moving slowly along the road.

In the evenings, she writes poems, although she never mentions this at school, undecided as to whether it would make her appear interesting or odd. She realises the poems are melancholy. This is how she feels. At school she is one person but at home she is another.

She leaves her poems in her bedside drawer which is

full of scraps of paper and notepads containing her story openings. Someone will discover the drawer after her death, like Emily Dickinson's sister, Lavinia, who opened the wardrobe after Emily died and found hundreds of tiny poems written on the backs of envelopes, bits of newspaper and chocolate wrappers. Mrs Williams, her English teacher, told them all about Lavinia finding Emily's secret poems. In Nell's mind the poems fall from the top of the wardrobe and onto Lavinia's head, so that she stands surrounded by tiny scraps of paper in a bare room in Massachusetts in 1886.

After Nell's death, the drawer full of her own writing will be discovered and she will be instantly famous. *It's so sad that she was so talented yet died so young,* people will say. And when they think of Alice: *Oh, yes, she's the mother of the famous writer, Eleonora Mae.*

Nell eats another spoonful of porridge then pushes the bowl away. She needs to be on time to meet her new friends at the lockers.

Isobel has large breasts and shapely legs. She tells Nell that her hair colour is chestnut and her bra size is the same as her mother's. Isobel's father works in finance. She has an older sister called Clementine who has her belly button pierced and whose boyfriend knows where to buy weed.

Carly is tall and a natural blonde. Her father is a farmer, and she has a younger brother, Samuel. Whenever

Carly mentions Samuel she rolls her eyes and calls him 'the royal pain in the arse'.

Zara has highlighted hair and a designer school bag. Her mother has a new boyfriend called Micky who wears a leather jacket. Micky plays lead guitar in a Stone Roses tribute band at the weekends. Zara's real dad lives in Birmingham and owns a restaurant. He takes Zara to have her hair done at Harvey Nichols when she goes to visit him which is apparently very expensive.

Isobel, Carly and Zara are the most popular girls in Nell's tutor group, and probably her year. She notices the way the other girls move out of the way when they pass. Nell does want to be like those girls; invisible, redundant, un-important.

The four of them choose who can sit at their table at lunch or stand with them in the playground. There are girls from other tutor groups who are occasionally allowed to sit at their table but they have to be carefully vetted, mostly by Isobel who seems to know everything about everyone.

Isobel, Carly and Zara did not go to Nell's primary school. A lot of the pupils from her primary went on to private or grammar schools. Nell did not go to a grammar school because Alice doesn't believe in them, and because she would have had to drive Nell in each day which would have cost a lot in petrol.

Nell's secondary school has a wide catchment area.

Many of the pupils arrive in coaches that pick them up from collection points in the morning. Nell's cottage isn't far enough away to warrant one of these coaches but it is far enough that Nell can take the regular bus in the mornings. Alice gives Nell money for the bus but Nell often prefers to walk, saving the one pound fifty. If she leaves early she can easily walk the couple of miles to the school, cutting across the fields to save time. Alice suggests Nell ride her bike to school like Grandma but Nell refuses. 'Only geeks ride bikes to school,' Isobel once said.

There are unspoken differences between those who arrive on coaches and those who walk or are driven to school by their parents. Those who walk or are driven to school live in, or close to, the villages. Those who get the coach are from the new estate several miles away. The coach children live in small, red brick, newly built houses. Their fathers work in factories or fix cars. The children who are driven to school belong to parents who are doctors, farmers or businessmen like Isobel's father who is always away. These children have bookcases and piano lessons. They go abroad during the summer holidays. They eat mussels and visit chateaux or, in Isobel's case, Disneyland.

Isobel, Carly and Zara are all from the villages. This gives them an air of above-ness which makes it easier for them to be popular.

Nell is an anomaly. She can talk about books and films but she has never been abroad or eaten mussels. The cottage is small and has no piano. She must rely on, or create, other attributes about herself so that she will continue to be accepted by her new friends.

Isobel knows all the gossip. She tells them about a Year Eight called Cherry who had been popular until she went to a Sixth Former's house one lunchtime when his parents were at work. She'd showed a friend a stain on her school shirt and the friend, who turned out to be not much of a friend, had told a few people who had told a few more people. The boy had been the wrong type of boyfriend, or else Cherry had done the wrong type of thing. Either way, she ended up having to change schools. Isobel had shaken her head. 'My sister said she was a real slut. Nobody was sad when she left.'

Isobel thinks it cool that Alice is an artist and that Nell grew up in London. Nell doesn't say anything to change Isobel's opinion. 'We couldn't even go out at night,' she tells Isobel. 'There were people doing drugs in the stairwells. Yeah, the area we lived in was really bad.' Nell isn't sure if these statements are entirely true but they are somewhere near the truth.

'Cool,' Isobel said. 'Your mum, she's kind of famous, isn't she?'

'She used to know a lot of famous people.'

Nell thinks of Alice's friends who turned up at the London flat: artists, writers, musicians. She remembers how they would talk and drink all night and how Alice would walk around in the mornings barefoot, wrapped in a threadbare blanket, throwing away empty beer bottles and emptying ash trays. The idea that this had been something 'cool' had never occurred to Nell until now. Alice's London friends have dissolved into hazy memories for Nell, but perhaps for Alice too.

'And you don't know who your father is?'

'No.'

'He could be a rock star or anything,' Isobel had said, thoughtfully, chewing the end of her ponytail.

Nell had shrugged. She can't explain to Isobel that her father is an unmentionable subject.

Isobel had been watching her, and Nell felt her hands twitching the way they do when she feels anxious and needs to scratch her arm. Instead she had reached into the pocket of her blazer and pulled out a pot of lime-flavoured lip balm.

'I had one of those. Only mine was grapefruit.'

'I nicked it from Boots.' Now this was definitely not true. Nell had bought the lip balm with last week's bus money, but once she had told Isobel this, she wasn't sure how to take it back.

Isobel had smiled and linked her arm through Nell's. 'Come on. Let's go and get chips for lunch. You can give me one of your Polos afterwards. I don't want stinky breath for history, I sit next to Ryan Hill.'

And so Nell had become a friend of Isobel's, and therefore Carly and Zara's too. Now all she has to do is make sure things stay this way. She can't help wishing Rachel was at her new school. Although she feels safe being a part of Isobel's group, she can't shake the feeling that she'd be even safer if Rachel were here.

Nell takes her porridge bowl over to the sink. She reaches for her bag and school pumps. She can no longer hear Alice moving around which means she must be working. Nell pauses in the hallway, knowing she should call out and say goodbye. Instead she slips quietly out the door.

18

Saturday. They have walked along the canal to get away from the town centre. There are boats with names like *Lisa Rose* and *April Star*. The air is scented with wood smoke and damp leaves. Isobel offers Nell her bag of Skittles but Nell shakes her head.

When she arrived, the others had already been around the shops. Alice was teaching a life-drawing class in the kitchen and had been unable to give Nell a lift into town. Nell had said a polite hello to the three students standing behind their easels, avoiding meeting the eye of the cold-looking naked woman sitting on the chair. Why can't they eat toast and jam in the kitchen on a Saturday morning without there always being a naked person sitting in the middle of the room?

'Look what we've got already,' Isobel had said when she'd arrived. Nell peered into Isobel's purple rucksack. It was full of items the girls had stolen: jewellery, make-up, coloured tights, hair serum, an eyelash curler, a pink bra and several pairs of knickers from Miss Selfridge.

'What will you do with all that?' Nell had asked.

'I don't know.'

'Won't your mum find it?'

Isobel laughed. 'I've got so much stuff. She won't notice.'

Carly looked at Nell. 'Now it's your turn. It isn't fair otherwise.'

Isobel had nodded, impressed with Carly's suggestion.

'Apparently you're the best at this,' Zara said. 'Isobel told us.'

'I'm not really.'

Isobel glared at Nell whilst zipping up her rucksack. 'Oh come on. You stole that lip balm, remember?'

Why had she said that? It had felt like something interesting to say, something Isobel would approve of. She could not say, now, that she hadn't stolen the lip balm, that she had saved her bus money for it.

'We'll stay here,' Isobel told her, 'whilst you go and get something.'

Nell entered the shop the others had chosen for her, an independent called Bow-jangles, and wandered around pretending to look at skirts and sparkly jumpers. Her legs were shaky, her breath coming out quick. The woman who owned the shop had smiled at her. 'I've got some new bits and pieces over the back, love. Pretty dresses for a Christmas party.' Nell couldn't bring herself to return the smile. She'd mumbled a thank you, waited until the woman had gone to help someone in the fitting room before slipping the small silver bracelet up her sleeve. She'd kept walking, all the time expecting the woman, another shopper, or the police, to come running after her. By the time she reached the others she'd felt sick and hot. Her hands were clammy. She'd felt particularly bad stealing from an independent shop. *That shop is someone's livelihood* she could imagine Alice saying.

'At least you got *something*,' Isobel said, holding the bracelet up so the others could see. 'We'll add it to the bag anyway. Try to do better next time.' Isobel dropped the bracelet into her rucksack. 'Come on. Let's walk along the canal.'

Carly takes the bag of Skittles from Isobel and empties a few into her hand, carefully so as not to take any purple ones. Those are Isobel's favourites.

'Let's have a look at everything then,' Zara says.

Isobel tips the plastic bag upside down and the contents fall onto the patchy brown grass. Zara picks up a pair of tights. 'We don't need these,' she says, throwing them into the canal. 'My mum buys me loads of these for school.'

Nell looks at the expensive Miss Selfridge tights floating on top of the water.

Isobel laughs. 'You're such a nutter, Zara.' She picks up a pair of red knickers and pings them at Zara who catches them and throws them over her shoulder. The knickers land in the muddy verge. They are a deep red with a lace trim and look startling against the brown, damp grass.

163

'Does anyone want this?' Isobel waves an eye shadow palette at them.

Carly shrugs. 'I'll take it. I've got one similar, but if no one else wants it…?' She glances at Nell who shakes her head.

Isobel is holding a bra from Debenhams – a thick satin with a leopard print trim. Nell would like to be the sort of girl who would own a bra like this.

'I'll never get these bad boys in this thing,' Isobel says, holding the bra against her chest and making a face. The others laugh and Nell joins in. Their laughter cuts through the cool crisp air causing a brown duck to take off from the water.

'I might have needed this when I was, like, ten,' Isobel says.

Nell watches as Isobel balls the bra up in her hand and throws it into the bushes where it gets caught in the green spiky leaves. She then shoves the remaining items: a lipstick, eyelash curler, feather earrings and hair serum back into the carrier bag. 'Come on,' Isobel says, brushing her hands on her jeans. 'Let's go for food.'

When they reach McDonald's, Nell announces she will just have some small fries.

'I thought we could get meal deals,' Isobel says, looking at the menu board.

'I don't feel hungry.' Nell thinks of the bracelet in Isobel's bag, the bracelet she stole.

'Nell always just has fries,' Carly says. 'It's why she's so skinny.'

'I'm buying everyone milkshakes,' Isobel says, pulling a twenty pound note from her purse. 'And I'll get you a burger, Nell. Don't worry.'

'It's fine, really—'

'I wish my parents gave me that much pocket money, they're so stingy.' Carly looks longingly at Isobel's twenty pound note.

'Oh, this isn't pocket money. Although I get enough.' Isobel folds the note slowly in half. 'I took this from my mum's purse this morning.'

'I can't believe you get away with that,' Zara says.

Isobel tilts her head and smiles. 'I started with a couple of quid. Then I took a fiver, then a tenner. I'm working my way up to a fifty.'

Nell knows she is supposed to feel impressed. She can't imagine taking money from Alice without asking. But what about the bracelet she stole earlier? She is no different.

Once Isobel has bought everyone food and milkshakes, they find a table. The girls talk about a boy in their tutor group called Billy, whose dad apparently gives him pornographic magazines.

'He's got a stack of them under his bed,' Zara says. 'His dad gives him his old ones.'

Carly makes a face. 'That's totally minging.'

'Yeah,' Isobel says. 'I bet all the pages are stuck together.'

Carly and Zara are both in hysterics. 'I almost choked on my chips,' Zara splutters.

The girls are talking too loudly. Nell pulls her bobble hat down low and squirms in her chair. She wishes they would talk quietly, or, even better, change the subject.

When, finally, ready to go, they leave their rubbish strewn across the table instead of taking it to the provided bins. Nell begins to tidy up, screwing up a burger wrapper and shoving it inside a chip box but Isobel stops her. 'What are you doing?'

Nell reluctantly leaves the rubbish where it is.

Outside, it's raining: a barely there, November rain. Nell pulls the hood of her coat up over her hat and follows the others as they head to the payphone. Zara has to be home because her grandparents are coming over for dinner. Carly is staying at Isobel's house tonight, and so Isobel calls her dad who will collect Isobel and Carly from the swimming pool car park.

When it's her turn, Nell slips into the phone box and closes the door behind her. Outside, the others are sharing a cigarette.

'This will be my last fag before Monday,' she can hear Zara moaning. 'My mum checks my pockets when she smells it on my clothes. She never asks if I've been smoking, only if I've "been up the chimney again." I'm fed up with it.'

'They think they're so funny,' Carly says.

'She needs to get a life.'

Nell dials home, dropping her twenty pence into the slot.

'Hello?'

'It's me. Can you pick me up?'

'Sure,' Alice says. 'I love being your private taxi. Where are you?'

Nell tells Alice to wait at the back of the library. She instructs her to arrive half an hour after she knows Isobel and Carly are going.

'Won't the swimming pool car park be easier?' Alice asks.

'No,' Nell says. 'I'm at the back of the library.'

Nell doesn't want to risk Alice arriving before Isobel's dad. She doesn't want the others to see Alice getting out of Grandma's ancient car in her heavy boots, corduroy trousers and paint-splattered jumper. She is sure Alice will wave at her and she knows she will die of embarrassment if she does.

'I have to go to the back of the library,' Nell says when she emerges from the phone box.

'Is your mum collecting you from there?' Zara asks.

'Yes.'

'She doesn't call her *Mum* she calls her *Alice*,' Carly says.

'But why *do* you call her Alice?' Zara asks.

Nell realises she does not have a ready-made answer to this question. 'I guess because when I was younger everyone else called her Alice, so I did too.'

Isobel laughs. 'You're so weird, Nell.'

Nell smiles. She has amused Isobel and it is good to be amusing.

After the others leave, Nell checks the time on her watch. She's got twenty minutes. She walks quickly out of the town centre and along the canal. The bra is still there in the bush. She reaches in and carefully pulls it out. The material is snagged in a few places but otherwise it is okay. She folds the bra, puts it in her coat pocket, then makes her way to the library.

'Did you have a nice afternoon with your friends?' Alice asks when Nell gets in the car.

'It was fine.' She stares out of the window wishing Alice wouldn't talk to her. She has secrets from Alice now. Alice would never understand why she stole the bracelet. She doesn't understand about school, about girls.

As they pull away from the curb, Nell watches a young mother with a buggy exit through the library's sliding doors. The woman struggles with the plastic cover, trying to pull it down over the wriggling toddler.

'What did you get up to?' Alice asks.

'We just went around the shops and looked at things.'

'Window shopping?'

'Yep.' She keeps her hand on the bra in her pocket. It feels soft and silky.

At home she tries the bra on in front of the mirror, turning her body so she can see herself from different angles. The under-wiring and padding make her breasts look bigger and more rounded, but Nell can see the red patches of skin on her arms and tummy. She is not beautiful. She is scratched and ugly. She is a freak. She does not look like any of the models in the magazines, or in the music videos she used to watch with Rachel. The models all have skin that is even and smooth; their hair is flat and shiny. Nell takes the bra off and hides it in the back of her drawer. She knows she will have to throw it away because Alice might find it and wonder where it came from. It was a stupid idea to go back for it. Still, for now, it is hers and she can't bring herself to get rid of it just yet.

19

When Nell is in her second year of secondary school, Alice finds a job. She responds to an ad in the local paper. *Cleaner wanted. Three mornings a week. Good hourly rate.*

No one has been to the cottage to look at Alice's paintings for a while. There are a lot of things Nell wants: new trainers for school, a mobile phone, pocket money. Nell does not like to ask for these things.

'I started my new job today,' Alice says at dinner.

Nell wants to finish her jacket potato so she can go upstairs and listen to the radio. That Alice has to do this job is insulting, somehow. Nell thinks of Rachel's cleaning woman, Magdeline, the way she could fold a T-shirt so it looked like it had just been bought from the shop. She can't imagine Alice folding a T-shirt like that.

'He works away a lot. I've never seen him. She doesn't work. They've got two children. Two girls. The youngest must be about your age. The Claytons?'

Nell puts her glass down on the table. 'What?'

Alice sighs. 'I was talking about the job. It doesn't matter.'

'You said the Claytons.'

'They're on Seabank Road. By the golf course.'

'You can't clean for the Claytons.'

Alice looks at Nell. 'Sorry?'

Nell breathes out noisily. She stares at Alice, her eyes cold and hard. 'Isobel Clayton. She's in my tutor group. I mean, she's my friend.'

Nell thinks of Isobel, the way she tosses her hair over her shoulder when she's about to speak. How she wrinkles her nose when something, or someone, displeases her. *Did you see Amanda Drew's shoes? She was wearing velcro.*

'I didn't realise you were friends with Isobel Clayton.'

'Well, I am.'

'You've never mentioned her.'

'You'll have to find another job.'

Alice takes a sip of water. 'I can't just leave my job because you're embarrassed, Nell.'

'I'm not embarrassed.'

'I think you are.'

Nell picks up her fork. 'Fine. I really don't care what you do.'

'That's nice,' Alice says.

At school, Isobel says nothing. Nell wonders if she is even aware that Alice is cleaning her house three mornings a week. Perhaps, as Isobel is always at school, she hasn't realised.

On Thursday, Nell is standing with the others on the field at break time. It's bright but gusty. The wind blows across the playing field, through the short grass. They stand, huddled together. Nell stamps her feet to keep warm.

'So your mum's our new cleaning lady then,' Isobel says.

Carly and Zara exchange glances.

Nell shrugs, shoves her hands in her pockets. 'Alice needs to do something for a while. Until she sells another painting.'

'You can tell her I like the way she tidies my room. She wipes the make-up off my dressing table and she puts all my CDs back in their cases.'

Nell hates the thought of Alice wiping the make-up off Isobel's dressing table. She can feel her cheeks flushing, despite the cold.

'My mum says you can come over for dinner anytime,' Isobel says. 'She told me I should go through my wardrobe and see if I have any old clothes I don't wear anymore that you might like.'

Nell stares at a speck of mud on her right school pump. 'I'm alright for clothes,' she says quietly. She imagines Tabitha Clayton trying to give Isobel's old clothes to Alice. She pictures Alice gratefully reaching out to take the black bin bag of Isobel's cast-offs. *Thank you*, she'll say.

Nell shivers as the bell rings.

* * *

172

'Your mum's paintings are kind of weird.' Isobel stands in the hallway looking at a portrait of Nell when she was four. 'Is this one you?'

Who else would it be? 'I used to sit for my mum a lot when I was younger.'

'Does she still paint you now?'

'Sometimes.'

Isobel continues to stare at the painting. 'I hope she doesn't paint you naked now.'

'No, not now. Of course not.'

'This one is you too.'

It's another painting of Nell that Alice did when they were in London. Nell is wearing knickers and a grey hat. Isobel laughs. 'Your boobs aren't much bigger now than they were then. There's a lot of you,' Isobel says, scanning the wall. 'You're naked in loads of these, or just in your knickers.'

Nell can feel her pulse quickening. 'There was no one else around.'

Isobel continues to stare at the paintings. 'It's still kind of pervy.'

'Don't you have any pictures of you and your sister in the bath or anything like that?'

'Yeah, I guess so. But not on the wall where any old perv could see them.'

Nell had been dreading Isobel coming to the cottage. She'd carefully chosen an afternoon when she'd known

Alice would be out. Of course she'd worried about what Isobel would think of the cottage, and of Alice, but she hadn't thought about Alice's work being a problem.

Going to other girls' houses is part of the ritual of friendship, just like meeting in town on a Saturday to go to McDonald's or the cinema, and stealing from the shops. She knows it isn't enough, in secondary school, to have just one best friend. Best friends are for primary school. In secondary school there are only packs of girls, like wolves.

Nell has been over to Isobel's house several times. The first time, she went alone, without Carly and Zara. Being asked over to Isobel's house was a special privilege. It meant that Isobel wanted to spend time with her, *just* her. She remembers the envious looks on the faces of the others when Isobel had stood, brushing her hair, in the toilets one lunchtime and said, 'Hey, Nell, want to come over to mine after school?' She felt as though she'd been given a secret key. She was a fully-fledged member of Isobel's private club.

The house had a circular driveway with a stone statue in the middle. Two trees in pots stood on either side of the front door. Its insides were full of grey and glass: grey carpets, lighter grey walls, silver curtain poles, white rugs, crystal chandeliers and long silver-framed mirrors. The kitchen was so white Nell had been afraid to touch anything. Isobel had told Nell to get the lemonade glasses out of the cupboard and Nell had stared at the handle-less wall of white, unable to figure out how to get behind it. Isobel giggled. 'You just press.'

Nell had met Isobel's mother, Tabitha, when she'd arrived home from the gym. Tabitha had walked into the kitchen in pink leggings and a matching sports bra. Isobel rolled her eyes.

'My mum still thinks she's twenty-five,' Isobel had said, once Tabitha left the room. 'She's actually forty-six. How old's your mum?'

'She's thirty-four.'

'Yeah, she looks young. She'd be pretty fit, your mum, if she didn't wear all those baggy clothes. If you don't mind me saying.'

'I don't mind.' Although she did. It was okay for Nell to have opinions about Alice's appearance but for some reason it did not feel okay for Isobel to comment.

Isobel had been asking Nell for several weeks when she could come to the cottage and Nell had known the visit would be unavoidable. It was beginning to look odd that she hadn't had any of the girls over and Isobel would, of course, have to be the first.

'Don't worry, I know your house is small,' Isobel had said.

Now Isobel is standing in the cottage hallway, her school bag still on her shoulder, her skirt hitched up at the waist, looking at Alice's paintings and discussing Nell's nakedness.

In the living room, Isobel looks slowly and obviously around. Nell can see her taking in the bare floorboards, the sofa with the worn patches on the arms, the canvases stacked against the walls, the table where they eat, covered in drawing paper, pencils, tubes of paint and palettes. She watches Isobel's eyes as they scan the sink, full of mugs and paint brushes, the cupboard with the door hanging off, the forest of herbs on the windowsill, the peeling lino, and the art books stacked precariously on top of the cupboards. She knows Isobel is trying to take in every detail in order to later relay it to the others. Nell was Isobel's find and she can therefore claim ownership over Nell's exoticness.

Isobel picks up a tea cup with a yellow flower design that once belonged to Grandma.

'Everything is so old and tiny. I didn't know people still had things like this.'

'Let's go to my room.' Nell heads for the stairs.

On the landing, Isobel stops. 'Are these you as well?'

They are standing in front of the wall of black and white photographs Nell had helped Alice develop. 'Alice took those the summer we moved in.'

'You haven't got many clothes on in these either.'

'It was hot. I was seven.'

Isobel peers closely at the photograph of Nell in bed. 'You can see your eczema in this one.'

'I think that was the idea.'

'But why? I mean, people are supposed to look better in photographs.'

Nell struggles to find the right words to explain to Isobel why Alice would take these kind of photographs as opposed to another kind. 'It's just life,' she says finally.

In Nell's bedroom, Isobel sits on the bed and surveys the room. Nell can see her looking at the floorboards, the furniture, the thin curtains with the seventies meadow print, her deodorant and hair clips, the lack of stuff.

Isobel's room had been overflowing with clothes, make-up and electrical hair equipment. She'd had a blue lava lamp, a French style dressing table, a TV, and lots of posters of men with their shirts off that Alice would never allow Nell to put on the wall.

Nell wishes she'd taken her animal posters down. She can imagine what Alice would say about that: *So nature isn't cool now?* She joins Isobel on the bed, curling one leg awkwardly underneath her.

'You've got a lot of old books.'

Nell looks at her stack of secondhand books. 'I guess so.'

'That must be why you're so good at English. Mrs Williams loves you. She's got a massive lezza crush on you. Bet she'd like to see those naked photos of you.'

Nell shrugs. 'I don't think she likes me very much. I just like reading.'

She wishes she hadn't brought Isobel here. She feels her private space has been violated by Isobel's presence, and wonders why she keeps saying the wrong thing. It seems easier, somehow, in school, to say the right thing, to laugh along with the others. At school, Isobel is one of Nell's closest friends yet outside of school she can't think of anything to say to her. She hopes Isobel won't open her bedside drawer and discover her notepads. *Can you believe Nell writes poems?* If Isobel wants to see inside Nell's bedside drawer she will have to show her because friends are not supposed to have secrets. Isobel will see her hag stone and her book on California and the shells she found on the beach, objects that belong to her and only her.

'Do you have any snacks?'

Isobel means crisps or biscuits or tortilla chips. She doesn't have anything like that. 'We've got nuts.'

Isobel makes a face. 'I'm alright, thanks.'

'My mum needs to go shopping.'

This isn't true. Alice says snacking ruins meals and confuses the digestive system.

Isobel sighs and picks at her nail varnish. A small crimson flake lands on the duvet. Nell can tell Isobel is growing bored. She feels she should have provided better entertainment. Isobel reaches into the pocket of her blazer. 'Hey,' she says. 'Can I smoke out your window?'

20

The following week, Nell arrives home from school to find Alice curled up on the sofa clutching a cushion. Her shoes have been discarded on the rug and there is an untouched mug of tea on the coffee table.

Nell puts her school bag down. 'What's wrong?'

'I've been sacked.'

'What do you mean? For what?'

'For stealing.'

'Stealing?'

Alice increases her grip on the cushion. 'I didn't steal anything. Obviously.' She sighs heavily. 'Fifty pounds went missing from Tabitha's purse.' Alice looks down. She threads a cushion tassel through her fingers.

Nell perches on the sofa arm, trying to understand what Alice is saying. She pictures it: Tabitha Clayton telling Alice to sit down, perhaps in the grey living room, or at the white kitchen table; Tabitha, telling Alice she doesn't want the money back, that she understands how hard things must be for her. Then she'll tell Alice, as if she's doing her a favour, that she won't go to the police. *Not over fifty pounds*, she'll say, and of course she'll be thinking of Nell too. *I won't do that to you, Alice. I'm a reasonable person. Our daughters are friends.*

Nell imagines Alice standing, walking into the hallway, taking her coat from the Claytons' peg rail. Once Alice has left, Tabitha will shut the door and listen to the sound of the car starting in the street. Perhaps it will take Alice several attempts to start the engine, as it often does. Once she is sure the car has gone, Tabitha will shake her head then walk back along the hallway to the kitchen. Already, she'll be thinking of how she will tell her husband later that evening. *It was just awful,* she'll say. *One of the hardest things I've ever done. I told her I wouldn't go to the police, and I didn't even ask for the money back. It isn't about that, is it?* Mr Clayton will take a bite of his vegetable spring roll. He'll pat Tabitha's arm and tell her they'll find another cleaning lady, that he's sorry she's had a bad day but that he's proud of her for handling the situation. He'll be thinking about the phone call to his line manager in Zurich he needs to make after dinner.

The worst thing is that Isobel and Eleonora know each other at school, Tabitha will say. *And I'll have to tell the girls at the tennis club. Sandra's looking for a cleaning woman. I can't not say anything, it would be irresponsible of me.*

Nell does not need to tell Alice that she knows she didn't steal the money. What she isn't sure of is why she doesn't tell Alice that Isobel Clayton stole it. Instead, saying nothing, she picks up Alice's cold cup of tea, takes it over to the sink, begins to make her a fresh one.

When Nell reaches the lockers, Carly and Zara are already there. Three heads, three pairs of legs, six eye-lined eyes, like a mythical beast she has no chance of slaying. They all know. As they walk along the corridor towards the classroom, the boys give Nell curious sideways glances. *Everyone* knows.

'We need to talk,' Isobel says in her best grown-up voice. A few of the boys look over and nudge each other. 'At break time,' she adds.

In science, Nell draws a diagram of a plant cell. She watches the clock, wanting it to be break time, wanting to get it over with. She guides her pencil around the edge of her cell, creating the cell wall. She adds the nucleus and the little specks of chloroplast, copying carefully from the board. Isobel will tell her she's sorry she stole the money and Alice got the blame. She'll ask Nell not to tell her parents and Nell will promise she won't. Isobel will say they should forget the whole thing, forget that Alice ever came to clean her house. Nell will agree. Still, they'll both know that neither of them will ever *really* be able to forget. Whenever anyone mentions money, or stealing, or cleaning women, there'll be glances and small smiles between them that the others won't notice. Nell will keep Isobel's secret because that's what friends do. After they've spoken at break, Isobel will link her arm through

Nell's and everyone will know that Eleonora Mae is still Isobel Clayton's friend, therefore popular and normal, therefore *somebody*.

Nell does not want to think of Alice right now. Alice can get another job. Alice should not have taken the job in the first place. What was she thinking?

When the bell rings for break, Nell gathers up her books, slips off her stool and finds herself in the corridor with the mass of pupils heading to their lockers or the canteen.

Once they've put their books away, Isobel turns to Nell. 'Let's walk,' she says.

Carly and Zara stay on Isobel's side. They do not want to walk next to Nell when her status in the group is uncertain. Nell stares at the floor, her shoulders slumped. She feels, like Tess, she is being led to the gallows. *I'm ready*, she thinks.

Isobel stops outside an empty history classroom. 'In here,' she says. 'Quick.'

They sneak inside and Isobel pulls the blind down over the glass panel in the door. 'So my mum sacked your mum.'

Carly suppresses a giggle and Isobel shoots her a look that silences her. The three girls surround Nell. Like jellyfish, she muses, remembering a recent biology lesson. *A group of jellyfish is often referred to as a smack. A smack of jellyfish.*

'We need to make sure this doesn't affect our friendship,' Isobel says.

'I know.' Nell draws in a slow, steady breath. She is happy to agree with whatever Isobel wants. She stays perfectly still, treading water.

'My mum says I can still be friends with you if I like.'

Nell had expected as much.

'It wasn't your fault that your mum stole from us because you're poor.'

Nell's body tenses.

'We all know that's why, Nell. You don't need to be ashamed.'

'We all know,' Zara echoes.

'I'm not ashamed,' Nell says, her voice coming out louder than she thought it would.

Carly sniggers and Isobel sighs wearily as if Nell is boring her.

Nell thinks of Alice sitting on the sofa with the cold cup of tea.

'Alice didn't steal the money. You did. We all know you stole it. You said you were going to. You just don't want to tell your mum.'

Isobel's face flushes a deep scarlet. 'How dare you speak to me like that.'

Carly and Zara look from Isobel to Nell. They were not expecting this. Neither was Nell. She has no idea where this fierceness has come from. All she knows is

183

that Alice did not steal the money and that Isobel should admit what she did. She can feel her heart racing. Her fists are clenched.

'I didn't steal anything,' Isobel says. 'I'm not *poor*.'

Nell's fist makes contact with the side of Isobel's face. Isobel reacts quickly and Nell feels Isobel's hand cross her cheek, her feet kicking at Nell's shins. She tries to fend off Isobel's slaps and punches with her arms but Isobel reaches for Nell's hair, yanking her sideways. One of the desks topples over as Nell crashes into it. She pushes back and slams Isobel against the whiteboard, grabbing at her ponytail.

'Get off me you bitch,' Isobel screams.

The door opens and the deep, booming voice of Mr Dennison, the history teacher, breaks their struggle. 'Stop that right now!'

Nell stands against the desk, using one hand to support herself. She can taste blood from her lip. Isobel's hair is sticking up, her shirt is untucked and her blazer has slipped off one shoulder; she has a small cut above her left eye. Nell smiles. Mr Dennison is saying that he doesn't need this now and what the hell were they doing in his classroom anyway? He sends them both straight to the deputy head.

'She started it,' Carly says, pointing at Nell.

Alice drops her car keys onto the kitchen table making a loud clattering sound. Nell takes her school pumps off and, for once, puts them neatly together in the hallway. She walks towards the stairs.

'Wait,' Alice says.

Nell turns around. She slumps onto the sofa, folding her arms across her chest. Alice goes into the kitchen where she puts the kettle on and runs the tap. Returning with a cold flannel, she hands it to Nell. 'Put this on your lip. It will help with the swelling.'

Nell takes the flannel and looks at the Driftwood Man sculpture Alice made the summer they moved to the cottage. She dabs at her sore lip, despising the blank, flat face, pointy chin and spindly arms. Still, she remembers collecting the driftwood on the beach, the waves rolling in, the wind biting her cheeks and, for a moment, wishes she could be seven again. This is ridiculous. She is thirteen and can never be seven again. She can hear Alice in the kitchen opening the fridge for milk. *She hates me.* Nell watches a tiny spider slowly climbing along the edge of one of Alice's canvases. She has an urge to squash it. She is not normally cruel like that.

Alice had arrived at reception in her paint-splattered clothes, old boots, gold hooped earrings; her hair tied back in her favourite red scarf, the scarf she wears when she's painting. The receptionist had raised an eyebrow. Alice followed the deputy head into his office, emerging five minutes later. Nell had stood, and the two of them had walked to the car park where they'd got silently into the car.

185

'They've suspended you for two days.'

Nell had shrugged, pulling her seatbelt over her shoulder.

She was strangely annoyed with Alice for not being more angry. Any other mother would have shouted, demanded to know what had happened, told Nell she would be grounded for a week. Alice only asked if Nell was okay, if her lip hurt. She'd put the radio on in the car and hummed along to a song from the eighties.

Alice brings the two mugs of tea in and puts them on the coffee table. She sits on the old flowery armchair opposite Nell, leaning forward slightly, resting an elbow on her knee and cupping her chin in her hand. 'He told me you hit the other girl first.'

Nell presses the flannel against her lip. Good. Alice doesn't know the fight was with Isobel Clayton.

'Was it about a boy?'

'No.'

'Are you sure?' Alice asks. 'Because if it was about a boy—'

'I said it wasn't, didn't I?'

'Then why are you so angry?'

Nell shrugs. 'It wasn't about a boy, okay?'

'Okay,' Alice says, holding her hands up.

Nell scratches at her arm.

'Try not to scratch.'

Nell stops scratching and glares at the wall. The spider has gone.

'Will things be okay for you at school? Will you make up with the other girl?'

Nell cringes. Alice is talking as if Nell is five years old, as if her and Isobel will hug each other tomorrow in the playground, hold hands and be best friends again.

'Things will be fine,' she says, closing her eyes. She listens to the sound of the clock ticking. She can hear Alice moving, the rustle of paper. When Nell opens her eyes again, Alice is sketching her. Nell wants to walk away, to tell Alice she has no right to draw her today with her cut lip and dishevelled hair, but she can't. It's like a muscle memory. All she has to do is keep still, and so she does, until Alice says quietly, 'That's it. Thank you.'

21

When Nell returned to school the girls ignored her. Nell tried to talk to Carly, to ask if she could arrange a time to speak to Isobel, to call a truce. Carly just laughed and said, 'She wouldn't be seen dead talking to someone like you.'

Nell discovered there was no longer a place available for her at the lunch table. As she approached, Zara wrinkled her nose. 'Do you smell something?' she'd said, causing Isobel to smile and Carly to giggle. 'It smells rotten.'

Nell had left her science classroom one afternoon to go to the toilet and when she returned her pencil case was on the floor, the pencils broken, her ruler snapped in half and her fountain pen leaking. The teacher hadn't noticed.

The boys bumped into her in the corridors, causing her to drop her books. 'Whoops. Didn't see you there.' She had to retrieve her books from the floor whilst trying not to get trampled on in the busy corridor.

The girls in Nell's year begin to whisper about her. *Freak, nutter, bitch, weirdo,* they say when she passes them in the corridors.

In geography, Carly complained that her purple pen was missing.

'Have you checked Eleonora's bag?' a tall, freckled boy called Joe Skipworth said loudly from the back of the room.

The girls erupted into giggles.

'Leave her alone,' Robbie Lock said, swinging back on his chair.

Nell had shot Robbie a look. She did not want anyone sticking up for her. They'd only tease him.

Nell has seen plenty of fights between boys in the playground but girls do not often hit other girls. When boys fight, it is forgotten the next day. When girls fall out, it is long and tormented and sometimes forever. Girls sneak up on one another with whispered words and turned shoulders. Girls work slowly, stripping away the thin layers of self-esteem, leaving a person feeling as though they've been hollowed out, like a pumpkin ready for Halloween.

Nell knows her friendships with Isobel, Carly and Zara will never be restored. She knows she will never again be popular. She will not be invited into town on a Saturday, to sleepovers, or the cinema, or to birthday parties in cold barns or village halls. There is a small part of her that feels a sense of relief. She no longer has to try.

Now, she spends her lunch breaks in the library, or reading at the back of the sports hall.

Each day, as she walks across the fields, she wonders what would happen if she didn't go to school, if she got on a bus to the station and took a train somewhere. She knows it is likely she would be found and returned. She is too young to go unnoticed. She also knows she could never put Alice through the stress of such a disappearance. She imagines Alice looking at the clock at five, wondering where she is and why she's late. She'll assume she's gone into town with her friends, or to someone's house after school and forgot to use the phone. By seven, there will be two plates on the table for dinner. *Where is she?* Alice will wonder, thinking of the dark watery dykes and then of the thirteen-year-old girl from Cheshire who went missing last year from the bus station and whose remains were found in the woods two months later. The story had been frequently on the news. CCTV footage of the girl showed her walking along the road the afternoon she went missing. In the next image, further along the same road, she was gone. The evening they'd announced the girl's remains had been found, Alice had turned the TV off. 'I'm sorry,' she'd said. 'I can't watch it.'

One afternoon, on her way home from school, Nell finds a dead rabbit on the path by the field. The rabbit has no eyes, just two hollow sockets. For some reason, she begins to cry. It happens frequently after that, the crying after school.

At home, Nell dries the dishes after dinner and irons

her school shirts. She completes her homework and cleans her shoes.

Alice watches her carefully. 'You don't go out with your friends much anymore.'

'They're all busy,' Nell says. 'Anyway, I've got homework.'

At night, Nell begins to dream. Her dreams are scary and have an absence of colour. There is an unseen entity that lifts her and throws her down the stairs.

She dreams of Driftwood Man. He has grown taller than the house. He taps on her bedroom window and reaches in with his giant and gnarled driftwood arm, groping around inside the room. Nell flattens herself against the wall as the huge wooden hand brushes past her. The hand retreats, and then there is an eye at the window, a single, monstrous eye with a hole in the middle. The hand reaches in again and grabs Nell so tightly she feels the air being squeezed from her lungs and she hasn't time to scream.

Nell wakes. Terrified, she creeps out of bed and across the landing. She opens Alice's bedroom door. Alice sits up, blinking. She's wearing her thick winter pyjamas, dotted with blue flowers.

'What is it?'

'I had a nightmare.' Nell stands in the the doorway feeling both frightened and stupid. She wants to tell

Alice how bad things are at school. She wants Alice to reassure her that she doesn't have to go back. Maybe Alice can teach her how to use the camera and they'll make photographs together again, just like they used to.

Alice switches on the bedside light and Nell tiptoes further into the room. She perches uneasily on the edge of Alice's bed.

'Do you want to talk about it?' Alice reaches for Nell's hair and strokes it gently. For once Nell doesn't flinch away.

'Driftwood Man.'

'My sculpture?'

'I was frightened of it when I was younger.'

'You should have said.'

'No. It's a good sculpture.'

'Is that what your nightmare was about?'

Nell stares at the faded pink stripes on the duvet cover. 'He was bigger than the house. He reached in through the window.' Now that she has told Alice, her dream sounds silly.

'It isn't a good sculpture,' Alice says thoughtfully. 'I've never liked it.'

Nell knows this isn't true.

'Let's go downstairs. It's good to get up for half an hour anyway. Then you'll be able to sleep again.'

In the kitchen, Alice puts the kettle on. 'It's weak,' she tells Nell. 'You don't have to drink all of it. Grandma used to say sugary tea is the best thing for shock. I've put a quarter of a teaspoon in.'

Nell takes the mug from Alice and holds it in her lap, feeling its warmth against her tummy. It's strange to be in the living room in the middle of the night.

Alice sits next to Nell on the sofa and sips her tea. She looks at Driftwood Man on the mantelpiece, puts her mug on the coffee table and quickly stands. 'Let's get rid of him.'

Nell watches as Alice twists sheets of newspaper for kindling and builds a fire in the grate. The logs are dry and burn easily. The clock chimes for two thirty as Alice hands Nell the sculpture. 'You do it,' she says.

'Are you sure?'

'I'm sure.'

Nell places Driftwood Man in the fire and they sit together on the sofa watching the flames engulf him, watching him burn. The logs crackle and hiss as Driftwood Man's face disappears.

Alice brings their duvets downstairs so they can be cosy. They don't talk, only sip tea and watch the flames leaping behind the grate.

Part Four

22

2000

Nell sits huddled on the sports hall steps, one hand holding her book, the other shoved deep into her pocket. It's February. Cold. The sky is paper white and the trees beyond the field are bare. She zips her coat up to her chin and fiddles with an old bus ticket inside her pocket. Absorbed in her book, she doesn't notice the two boys until they are upon her.

'Hey,' Robbie says.

Nell looks up. Robbie is with a boy from the year above – Darren Kingsley. Darren is tall and intense with dark hair and grey eyes. She is surprised to see Robbie with Darren. Darren is somehow both popular and a loner. Nell isn't sure how he manages to achieve this contradiction. He has the respect of the other boys in his year, or perhaps they are wary of him. He plays basketball, this is all she knows.

'How's it going, Nell?' Robbie asks, shuffling his feet.

'Okay.'

'You'll get cold sitting here.'

'I'm fine.' She returns her gaze to her book, hoping they will go away.

Without being invited, Darren Kingsley sits next to her on the step. Nell can smell his deodorant mixed with stale cigarette smoke and something else, something oily. He takes a packet of cigarettes from his blazer pocket and offers her one.

She shakes her head, looks away.

'Robbie doesn't smoke,' Darren says, gesturing towards Robbie who stands awkwardly, leaning against the wall. 'He's got asthma. But I thought you might.'

Nell shrugs. 'I guess I do. When the mood takes me.'

'When the mood takes me,' Darren repeats slowly. 'I like that.' He looks across the school playing field and Nell fiddles with the hem of her skirt. She's never been this close to a boy in Year Ten before.

'And just when does the mood take you, Nell?'

Nell can feel her cheeks reddening. She wasn't even aware he knew her name.

'Robbie tells me you're in his tutor group.'

'Yes.'

'He says you're a swot.'

Robbie looks sheepish. 'I meant it in a nice way.'

'Only at English. I'm rubbish at everything else.' This isn't true but she says it anyway.

Darren studies her carefully and Nell shifts on the step, edging away from him. His gaze makes her feel uncomfortable although it is also, strangely, quite thrilling to have a person look at you in this way.

'Didn't you once beat up that stuck-up cow Isobel Clayton?'

He mentions the fight as if it has given Nell some credibility. 'Yeah,' she says. 'I did.'

'And you spend your lunch breaks alone?'

'I guess so.'

Darren flicks his lighter several times until he gets a flame. 'You're a bit crazy, aren't you?'

Nell smiles uncertainly but Robbie frowns.

'I like this spot you've chosen,' Darren says, putting the lighter back in his pocket. 'Nice and quiet.'

'That's why I like it.'

From somewhere far away the bell begins to ring. A few crows take off from the field, squawking loudly.

'We should hang out sometime. I'll take your number.'

Nell looks over at Robbie but he's shaking his head and staring at his shoes.

'I'm really glad Robbie introduced us,' Darren says, following her gaze. He takes his phone from his pocket – a brand new Motorola. He flips it open and Nell reads him her home number.

'You don't have a mobile?'

'Not yet.'

Darren shrugs. 'This will have to do then.'

The three of them cross the courtyard together and

Nell smiles to herself. *If only Isobel, Carly and Zara could see me now. Walking across the courtyard with Darren Kingsley from Year Ten.*

The following day, after school, Nell is cutting up an apple in the kitchen. Alice isn't home yet – she's been teaching a class. Nell sweeps the core of her apple, along with two pips, into the container Alice keeps for peelings. She jumps when the phone rings.

'Hello?'

'Hello Nell.'

It takes Nell a moment to work out who it is. No one ever phones for her anymore.

'Are you surprised I've called you?'

'No,' she lies.

'Good. Listen, it's Year Ten parents' evening tomorrow.'

'Is it?' Nell wonders if Darren is worried about parents' evening. She can't imagine Darren Kingsley being very popular with the teachers. 'I'm sure it will be fine,' she says.

'Yeah. Anyway, it's straight after school. My parents have an early slot. Why don't you meet me? You can hang out with me whilst I wait for them.'

Nell wonders briefly about the logistics of this. If she isn't home on time Alice will wonder where she is. Nell will have to tell her, in the morning, that she is staying late at school. Alice will ask why. She can't say detention as Alice will want to know the details. She can't say she wanted to stay for netball practice or band practice. She isn't particularly good at sports and has never played anything more than the recorder when she was nine.

'I'll meet you in the courtyard after school,' Darren tells her.

Nell grips the receiver. 'Okay.' She will figure out her excuse for Alice later.

'I'm really looking forward to being able to spend time alone with you.'

Nell imagines Darren watching her at school, wanting to talk to her, to spend time alone with her. The thought is exciting.

'I want to spend time with you too.'

'I thought so,' Darren says. 'I felt a connection.'

Nell stares at her slices of apple browning on the chopping board.

'See you tomorrow. The red bench in the courtyard.'

'Sure,' Nell says, but Darren has gone.

Alice enters through the back door carrying a string bag full of shopping and Nell drops the phone. She quickly reaches to retrieve it.

Alice puts the bag on the kitchen counter. 'What's up with you? You jumped out of your skin.'

'Nothing,' Nell says, putting the phone back on its cradle. She returns to her apple.

'Who was on the phone?'

'Just a sales call.'

Darren has the keys to his parents' car. 'We've got about an hour,' he says. They walk silently across the courtyard towards the car park. Nell has told Alice she is attending a study group after school, additional notes for *A Street Car Named Desire*. It's only four o'clock but already the light is fading. The sky is streaked pink and gold over the playing field. Nell breathes into her hands to warm them.

'We'll have more privacy in here.' Darren opens the rear door of the car and gestures for Nell to get inside. 'And it's warmer.'

'Thank you.' Relived to be out of the cold, she climbs in and scoots across to make room for Darren who pulls the door shut behind them. He gazes at Nell and brushes a strand of hair from her face, tucking it behind her ear. The gesture is possessive; she is something Darren has the right to examine, to tidy up. He leans forward and kisses her, crushing his lips against hers. The kisses are big and wet. Being kissed by Darren is not like when she practised kissing the mirror in Rachel's bedroom. Mirrors don't kiss back, they don't try to swallow your tongue. Nell isn't entirely sure this is what she wants but she feels it is too late now to change her mind. She said she was okay with sitting in the car and it was probably her fault for not understanding that sitting in the car meant kissing. Without the kissing she will not be considered, and although she isn't sure exactly what Darren Kingsley is considering her for, she wants it all the same.

Darren pulls away from her and she gasps for breath. He winds the window down, letting some air in. 'Most guys would have had a hand in your knickers by now,' Darren says. 'But I'm not like that.'

Nell glances at the car door handle. She nods, wanting to reassure Darren that she knows he is a good person. Her lips feel tingly. She touches her bottom lip with her thumb. Her chemistry teacher, Mr Parr, crosses the car park with his briefcase. He doesn't look in their direction.

Darren reaches for Nell, his hands hot and slightly damp. He pulls her awkwardly on top of him. She allows him to manoeuvre her in the way he wants until she can feel Darren's groin against her, a hard lump. Her breath quickens. She looks down at Darren, noticing the flecks of dandruff in his gelled hair. He's got an angry red spot forming on his forehead.

'This is one of the positions we could do if we had sex.'

Nell isn't sure what to say. The word sex, coming from Darren, sounds dangerous and grown up. Darren Kingsley is a person who knows about sex.

'Get up,' he instructs her. 'I'll show you another way.'

Darren makes Nell get on her hands and knees on the

back seats. He kneels up behind her and grinds his groin against her buttocks. 'This is a good one,' he says.

Like deers, Nell thinks. She's seen the male stags in the Scottish highlands on *Autumn Watch*, the way they mount the females.

'You can sit up now,' Darren says, so she does.

He leans back in the seat next to her and checks his phone. 'Let's get out. I need a cigarette.'

She climbs out of the car, her legs shaky. Darren follows. Standing by the car, Nell feels small, like she is shrinking into herself. She pulls at her coat sleeves.

'Why don't you come over on Saturday?' Darren asks, taking his cigarettes from his blazer pocket.

'To your house?'

He smiles. 'Yeah. Where else?'

Nell stands awkwardly, tugging at her skirt. 'Won't your parents mind?'

Darren shrugs. 'No. My dad will be out. My mum pretty much lets me do what I want.' He lights a cigarette.

'Okay.'

Darren nods, pleased. 'You need to get the number five bus to The Fox and Hounds. Here, I'll give you the fare too. Don't want you to be short.' He shoves a crumpled five pound note into Nell's hand.

'Thank you,' she says, thinking it nice of Darren to cover her bus fare.

'Great. See you Saturday then.'

Nell leaves Darren leaning against the car, smoking his cigarette. She crosses the road and makes her way over to the bus top, perching on the end of the bench, glancing at the board – good, there'll be a bus along in ten minutes. She sits on her hands, swings her legs, trying to keep warm. Her stomach feels knotted and she has the unshakeable sense of something not being right. *But I have made out in a car. I have made out with Darren Kingsley from Year Ten.* She straightens out the crumpled five pound note, folds it neatly, and slips it carefully into her purse.

23

By the end of the week it grows even colder. The mornings are heavy and still with thick February frost. The fields sparkle like they've been sprayed with a fine, glittery powder. Nell dresses quickly then goes downstairs. Alice is in the kitchen making toast under the grill.

'You're up early. Are you going out?'

'Just into town. To meet some friends.'

Alice smiles. 'Good. Aren't you having breakfast?'

'I'll get something later.'

Alice gives Nell five pounds from Grandma's chipped tea pot which is where she keeps cash for emergencies. 'Here. Take this.'

'Thanks,' Nell says, wishing Alice hadn't given her the money. She can't tell Alice that Darren Kingsley has already given her the bus fare.

Nell leaves the cottage, walks to the bus stop then takes the bus into town. She sits at the grey concrete terminus waiting for the next bus which will take her to the village where Darren lives. When it arrives, the bus is small, much smaller than the one she takes to school.

She boards, stepping up behind an elderly lady with

shopping bags. 'Do you stop at The Fox and Hounds?' she asks, remembering Darren's instructions.

'That's right, love. Want me to give you a shout when we're there?'

'Please. Thank you.'

She takes a seat, close enough to the front that she'll be able to hear the driver call her when it's her stop. She keeps her gloves on, gazes out of the window at the frost-covered fields and bare winter trees.

When she arrives, Darren is standing at the bus stop, smoking. Nell steps off the bus. He greets her with a nod and flicks his cigarette into the road. They walk together through the village and along a narrow dirt track. She feels privileged. Out of all the girls at school, he has chosen her. Darren's house is a red brick farmhouse with bags of sand and planks of wood leaning against the porch. There are several outhouses, and a quad bike hitched to a trailer. Nell hears the moo of a cow. 'You've got cows?'

'Yeah. They get milked twice a day. I do it before school with my dad. Robbie comes and helps out sometimes.'

'Can I see them?'

'What do you want to see a load of stupid cows for?'

Nell feels silly so says nothing. There is an upside down, wooden boat by one of the barns. The paint is peeling but Nell can make out the letters that spell *Caroline*.

'Me and Dad are going to fix her up,' Darren says as they pass.

Nell tries not to step in any of the frozen puddles. Closer to the house, an old Land Rover is parked next to a caravan. The caravan has a net curtain at its window and tufts of grass around its wheels. The door opens and a young bearded man appears wearing a hooded jumper and tracksuit trousers. He's lighting a cigarette. His eyes meet Darren's but Darren looks away.

'Who's that?' Nell whispers.

'Niko,' Darren says, as they cross the drive. 'He's Bulgarian. Been here a couple of weeks. My dad hired him. He'll stay for the spring. Moody bastard. Robbie's always hanging around him. I reckon they're bumming each other.'

Nell wishes Darren hadn't said it the way he did. She hopes he doesn't say things like that about Robbie at school. It wouldn't go down well.

'It must be freezing in that caravan,' she says finally.

Darren shrugs. 'Sure he's used to it.' He grins. 'And he's got Robbie to keep him warm.'

As they reach the house, Darren takes his keys from his pocket and opens the front door. Muddy wellies stand in the porch and, on the mat, a few letters which Darren kicks to one side. Nell steps into the hallway. The wallpaper is flowery and faded. A photograph of a grinning man holding a rosette and standing next to a large cow hangs on the wall next to another of a freckled girl in a primary school uniform. The girl has her hair in bunches and is missing a front tooth. An assortment of old coats hang from a peg rail. The house smells greasy, of roast chicken. Nell feels something soft against her jeans. A grey and white cat winds itself around her legs. Darren reaches down and gives the cat's back a pat. 'This is Bluebell. My little sister named her.'

'She's beautiful.'

'She had kittens last year. My dad drowned them in the water butt. We told Megan we'd given them away.'

Nell takes a step back. She feels a clenching in her stomach. 'Oh. Did you have to do that?'

Darren smiles. 'We couldn't keep them, Nell. Come on. Let's go say hello.'

Nell understands farm cats often have kittens that can't be kept but she wishes they really had been given away. She can't believe anyone could drown kittens. She would have liked a kitten, although she knows Alice wouldn't have agreed. Alice would say a kitten would step in her paints and wee up her canvases.

She follows Darren through to the kitchen where a small, tired-looking woman is unpacking shopping. She wears a dress that has a tiny duck print pattern, grey tights and a bulky cardigan. Her hair has been clumsily clipped back and strands of it escape around her ears.

The kettle is boiling, making a whistling noise. The greasy roast chicken smell is much stronger in the kitchen, although there is nothing in the oven.

'Hi, Mum.'

'Hello, love.'

Darren must look more like his father, perhaps the man in the cow photograph. Nell doesn't recognise many of his features in his mother. His forehead perhaps, his chin, but not his eyes. 'This is Nell,' Darren says, as if she requires no further explanation, and then, 'We'll be upstairs.'

'Okay, love,' Darren's mum is busy putting a bag of leeks into the bottom drawer of the fridge. 'It's nice to meet you, Nell.'

'It's nice to meet you too.' Nell feels she should say something more but Darren is already leaving, gesturing for her to follow.

The walls of Darren's bedroom are painted blue and grey. He has a wooden bed and a red and black striped duvet cover. An orange basketball sits on top of a large chest of drawers. In the corner stands a cabinet with glass doors. Inside the cabinet are several guns.

Darren notices her looking. 'Air rifles,' he says.

'Do you use them?'

'Yeah, of course I use them. I shoot rats around the farm, rabbits too sometimes.'

Nell shifts her weight from one foot to the other. Alice once told her Grandma ate a lot of rabbits in the war when meat was scarce. She suspects this is not the reason Darren shoots rabbits. 'Don't your parents mind?'

'No, why would they? They bought them for me. And these,' Darren tells her, pointing at the shelf below. 'These are replicas. This one's a Magnum, like Dirty Harry's, and this is a Desert Eagle. Micky Rourke used one of these in *Year of the Dragon*. Ever seen that film?'

Nell shakes her head.

'It's fucking great. Yeah, if I shot you with a real one of these it'd take your head off.'

Nell smiles weakly. She stares at all the guns, shifts her weight from one foot to the other. They make her feel uncomfortable, even though she knows they're fake.

'We've got a proper rifle of course. And shotguns. My dad keeps them locked up in the wardrobe.'

'Oh.'

'I had to shoot a calf last spring. It was born all funny.'

'Couldn't you have called the vet?'

Darren smiles at her. 'Vets cost money, Nell. She was fucked anyway. It was the kindest thing to do. I shot her right between the eyes.' He mimes shooting the calf. 'Lucky she wasn't a bull.'

He moves away from the cabinet and switches the TV on. It's an American basketball game. He must have Sky TV in his bedroom.

'You play, don't you?' Nell says, because it is something to say, and because she is grateful to be off the subject of guns and dead cows.

'Yeah,' Darren replies, his eyes on the screen.

Nell watches as a player jumps for the ball. The player turns and takes a shot at the basket, scoring.

'I play for county. I'm captain. I'll probably captain the senior team when I'm eighteen, if I haven't signed up by then. I'm getting out of this dump as soon as I can.' Darren glances scornfully out of the window then moves his gaze to the bed. 'Hey, why don't you watch the game with me here? It's more comfortable. Go on.'

Nell gets tentatively onto the bed. She moves over to make room for Darren who climbs on after her meaning she is now between Darren and the wall. She leaves a narrow space between their bodies like a fault line. Darren's closeness, his *boyness*, feels overwhelming. She looks at their blue jeaned legs stretched out on Darren's duvet. His legs are longer than hers. His big toe pokes through a hole in his thick woolly sock. The bed is pushed up against the radiator and she can see that the wallpaper behind it is peeling. Darren reaches under the bed and pulls out a packet of Doritos. He opens them and offers the packet to Nell. She takes a few even though she isn't hungry. She expects there will be more kissing but she isn't sure when the kissing will take place and this makes her anxious. She eats slowly and carefully, not wanting to crunch too loudly or get crumbs in the bed, although she notices Darren drops several. The Doritos stain her fingers orange. She tries to wipe them on her jeans without Darren noticing.

212

'I care about you, Nell. You know that, right?' Darren's eyes briefly leave the screen.

Nell nods, edging closer to the wall. Darren screws up the empty Doritos bag and tosses it under the bed. He leans across and kisses her much like before in the car. The kiss lasts a long time and Nell struggles for air. She can hear the roar of the crowd as something happens on the TV. Darren doesn't seem to notice. Perhaps he has lost interest in the game. He puts his hands on Nell's breasts, squeezes them gently through her clothes. Nell can feel her body tensing.

'Can I see them?' he whispers, close to her ear.

Nell looks at the TV screen. A whistle is blown and there appears to be a break in the game. The players are slinging towels over their shoulders and reaching for water bottles. They pat each other on the back. She slowly removes her jumper and T-shirt but not her bra, as if this might be enough.

Darren looks at her, his gaze steady. 'And your bra.'

Nell slides the straps of her white cotton bra off her shoulders. She long ago threw out the bra Isobel stole, the bra she retrieved from the bush. It hadn't felt right to keep it and she wasn't sure who she was when she tried it on. Now, though, she wishes she'd kept it. She wishes she'd gone back and stolen the matching knickers. She feels she should be wearing a different kind of underwear, that she is ill-equipped for this unexpected performance.

She can feel Darren's eyes on her as she slips the bra down over her breasts and pulls the clasp to the front, carefully undoing it then dropping the bra onto the bed. Darren studies her breasts but makes no move to touch them.

'Take off your jeans.'

Nell does as Darren says. Why she does this, she isn't sure. The option not to doesn't occur to her. Darren likes her. Darren *cares* about her. Darren is older. He knows things that she does not. She is in Darren's house eating Darren's Doritos whilst his mother, downstairs, puts the shopping away and makes a cup of tea. All of this is normal. Everything is okay. He even gave her the bus fare.

Darren is taking his jeans off. He throws them, along with his T-shirt and jumper, into a pile on the floor. His skin is pale, his legs are hairy. He is now wearing nothing but blue boxer shorts. He pulls Nell close to him. She can smell his deodorant and the Doritos on his breath. His skin against hers feels alien and she fights the urge to move away from him, digging her nails into the palm of her hand. *This is what people do*, she tells herself. She wonders if all this must mean Darren is now her boyfriend. The thought comforts her. She likes the sound of it – *my boyfriend*. She thinks of holding hands with Darren at school, of going to the cinema with him, of staying at his house for dinner. *I spent the weekend with my boyfriend*, she'll tell the girls at school.

Darren is reaching for her hand. 'Have you ever felt a cock before?'

Nell shakes her head. 'No.' Her voice comes out as a whisper.

He takes her hand and places it inside his boxer shorts. She knows what she is supposed to do from the rude hand gestures the boys make at school.

'That's it,' Darren tells her. 'Yeah, you're good. I reckon you've had practice, Nell.'

Nell giggles from nervousness. 'No.'

'That's what they all say.' Darren places his hand over hers. 'I want to touch you too,' he tells her pushing her knickers aside. His fingers are warm and clumsy. No one has ever touched Nell *there* before. She doesn't want it. She wants to move away, to clamp her legs shut, to make him stop. *But I touched* him, she thinks. She feels confused, lightheaded. All of this is happening to someone else.

'I'm gonna finger you,' Darren murmurs in her ear. 'It's okay. It'll feel nice.'

He pushes his finger inside her and Nell gasps. She didn't mean to cry out but it hurt more than she had thought it would. Darren is wriggling his finger around. It is strange, uncomfortable. Once again, Nell wants to move away, to find a way to make him stop, only she can't. Her throat feels tight and she has lost all of her words.

'Is that good, Nell?'

She stares at him.

Darren pulls his finger out. He's reaching for something from his bedside drawer. He holds the shiny foiled square and begins to rip it open.

'Sex is great,' Darren tells her. 'You'll love it. And it's easy. There's nothing to it. I'll show you.'

This is not what she imagined when she thought of spending Saturday at Darren's house. But what *had* she imagined? She wants to tell him that she doesn't feel ready, despite all the positions he showed her in the car, that she has only just turned fourteen, that she never imagined it to be like this. She had always thought 'losing her virginity' would involve candles and flowers and four-poster beds and a boy, nervous and grateful and in love. She had not imagined a single bed pushed against the wall, replica guns, a basketball game, Doritos.

'Trust me,' he tells her. 'You don't want to lose it with some dickhead when you're pissed at a house party in Year Eleven. You'll thank me for this. You'll never forget me.' He shuffles out of his boxer shorts, then takes the condom out of the packet and fiddles with it under the duvet. Nell is glad he didn't ask her to do it. She wouldn't want to get it wrong, for him to see that she doesn't know how to do it. She stares at Darren's TV, at a soft drinks advert. She feels numb, removed, although her heart is beating fast in her chest.

'Now you,' Darren tells her. 'Take your knickers off.'

Nell does as he says, her movements disconnected from herself. She lies naked under his red and black striped duvet.

Darren straddles her and Nell stares at his penis. She has seen naked men before. Alice sometimes uses male models at her life-drawing classes. She has seen the soft and squashy things between their legs. Darren's is different. It points aggressively towards her. She knows it is supposed to fit inside her but she can't think how it would be able to do so. It is much bigger than his finger.

Darren slowly moves Nell's legs apart and lowers himself on top of her. He pushes his penis against that private part of herself. 'Just relax,' he whispers. 'It's easier.'

And then there is the pain. It shoots through Nell making her gasp. She grips a handful of Darren's fitted sheet and clenches her teeth. Darren begins to thrust into her as if he hasn't noticed. He moves silently to his own rhythm. Nell screws her eyes shut. It hurts, but the pain is not as great as that initial, shocking wave. After what seems like forever, Darren makes a strange grunting sound and collapses on top of her. He slides himself out then sits up and fiddles with the condom.

Nell stares at the ceiling She has the urge to curl herself up into a tiny ball. She wants to be very small.

She wants to disappear. She looks at the TV screen where two men with microphones are talking and realises the players haven't yet returned to the court.

'Shit,' Darren says.

'What?' Nell sits up.

'The condom's split.' Darren glares at Nell as if this is her fault.

Nell's breath catches in her throat. Does this mean she'll be pregnant?

Darren shakes his head. 'For fuck's sake.' He throws the condom onto the floor.

'What do we do?' she whispers.

Darren looks at her like she's an idiot. 'You go and get the morning-after pill,' he says. Nell nods faintly. She feels sore and disorientated. All she had wanted to do was please Darren, to make him happy, or at least not let him down. All she has done is make him angry.

Darren is getting dressed so Nell does the same, finding her knickers, wriggling into her jeans, pulling on her T-shirt. Her hands are shaking and she tries to dress quickly.

'You'd better get it,' Darren says, zipping up his jeans. 'Remember the kittens.'

Nell sits on the edge of the bed. She thinks she might be sick.

'Go to the chemist this afternoon. Shit,' Darren says, staring at the bed. 'You've bled on my sheet too.'

Nell looks at the small, bright stain on the white crumpled sheet. 'I'm sorry,' she whispers.

Darren sighs. He reaches for his wallet and keys. 'Come on. I'll walk you to the bus stop.'

Nell had imagined she'd stay at Darren's house for dinner but it doesn't seem to matter now. She just wants to be out of this room.

On the way to the bus stop, Darren lights a cigarette. He offers Nell one but she declines, thinking it will make her feel more nauseous. A group of starlings appear. Nell watches as they swell and dip in the huge sky. She remembers the word Grandma taught her for a group of starlings: *murmuration*. A murmuration of starlings. The starlings are still here, Nell thinks, and when I get home maybe everything will be just the same as it was. One or two cars pass them, followed by a cyclist. The road is not busy. There is a cluster of snowdrops at the bus stop.

As much as she wants to be at home, to be away from here, she can't bear the thought that this is it, that Darren will never want to see her again.

'Will you call me?'

Darren shrugs. 'Yeah. Whatever.'

Nell watches Darren walk away. He grows smaller and smaller as he continues along the narrow, flat road back to his house with its roast chicken smell and blood-stained sheet. She watches him flick his cigarette butt into the dyke.

When the bus arrives, it's the same driver. He smiles as she steps on and shows him her return ticket.

'That didn't take long,' he says, cheerfully.

'No,' she replies.

Nell arrives home just after one. She takes a shower, running the water as hot as she can bear it. She washes her hair, scrubs her body, uses half a bottle of shower gel.

She steps onto the bathmat and reaches for her towel, wrapping it tightly around herself. The room is full of steam. She uses the palm of her hand to wipe the condensation from the door of the mirrored cabinet over the sink and stares at her reflection. *I am the same but different.* She remembers what Grandma used to say after she'd had a bath: *All clean?*

She sits down slowly on the edge of the bath and squeezes the water from her hair whilst looking at the painting of Alice: *Self portrait as a young girl.* Alice's huge eyes are looking ever so slightly off to the right. Nell doesn't like the painting. She wishes it wasn't in the bathroom. It feels like an invasion of her privacy. She can hear Alice ascending the stairs, probably wanting to use the bathroom. *Oh, go away.*

'Nell?' Alice calls out. 'I need to wee. Can I come in?'

Nell rolls her eyes.

The bathroom door opens before Nell has a chance to reply and Alice appears. 'Oh,' she says, looking at Nell.

Nell recognises Alice's expression, her need.

'Don't move.'

Nell wants to tell Alice that she isn't in the mood but Alice is running down the stairs. 'I'm not sitting for you here,' Nell calls after her.

Alice reappears a minute later with her pad and pencil. 'Just a quick sketch,' she says. 'Hold still. Look down, the way you were when I walked in.'

Nell clutches the towel and looks at the bathroom floor. She feels miserable and she wants to be alone. 'I'll get cold.'

'No you won't.'

'I thought you needed a wee.'

'I won't be long,' Alice says. 'I can hold it if you can.'

24

At the chemist, Nell waits behind a man with a wooden walking stick. She looks at the stand of Chupa Chups lollies, remembering how she used to wish Alice would buy her a strawberry and cream-flavoured lollipop and how Alice would say that sweets would give her holes in her teeth and turn them rotten. Nell already feels rotten. She'll be a teenage mother with no boyfriend and no GCSEs. She'll have to move somewhere far away, somewhere Darren will never find her and the baby. Alice will be ashamed of her. People will talk about them. *I heard the mother stole from the Claytons. Did you know her daughter's pregnant? She's only fourteen.*

'Can I help you?'

The man has gone and the pharmacist, a short-haired woman with dangly earrings, is looking at her.

Nell glances quickly around, making sure there is no one else there, before shuffling forward, keeping her eyes on the counter. 'I'd like to get the morning-after pill please,' she says quietly.

'Oh,' the pharmacist says, her eyebrows raising slightly. 'I'm sorry. You can't buy it from us. The doctor has to give it to you.'

Nell looks blank. Her palms are clammy and the pharmacist's face and the wall of medicine behind her are all blurred. She grips onto the counter for support.

'It's prescription only,' the pharmacist says, staring at Nell. 'I'm very sorry.'

'I'll go to the doctors then,' Nell mumbles, backing away from the counter.

'It's Saturday,' the pharmacist calls after her. 'There's a drop-in centre at the hospital. If you wait a minute I'll see if I can—'

But Nell is scared and she doesn't want to wait, to have to explain anything more. This task now feels way beyond her capabilities. She needs air, lots of air. She turns and heads for the exit.

As she moves towards the heavy door, she feels the panic rising in her chest, spreading through her body like wildfire, threatening to take over. The pharmacy with its shelves of creams, cotton wool and hair clips is foggy and out of focus. Her breathing is shallow and she can't seem to get enough air into her lungs. She rushes outside and collides with someone who is on their way inside.

'Whoa, Nell.' Robbie steps back onto the pavement. 'Hey, are you okay?'

Before Nell can stop herself, she begins to cry. Robbie reaches forward and attempts to comfort her, putting his arm on hers and steering her away from the pharmacy entrance.

'Sorry,' Nell sobs, her voice shaky. A tear slides down her nose.

Robbie blinks, unsure of what to do. 'It's alright,' he says. 'Let's sit down. Over there. It will be better if you sit down.'

They cross the road, Robbie's hand at Nell's elbow. They sit together on the bench by the pond.

Nell tries to compose herself but the situation feels hopeless. She takes in huge gulps of air.

'Nell, you're really worrying me.'

'I need to get the pill,' she manages to say.

'It's alright,' Robbie says. 'It's going to be alright.'

Robbie doesn't understand. Nell tries again. 'I need to get the morning-after pill. Darren told me to get it.'

'Oh.'

Nell can see Robbie thinking, realising, and this only makes her want her to cry harder. Even Robbie Lock won't want to be seen with her. She's nothing but a dirty slut, like Cherry, the girl who did something with a sixth former and had to move school.

Robbie stands and kicks the leg of the bench. 'Fuck. I hate that arsehole.'

Nell looks at Robbie, surprised by his anger on her behalf. She wipes her eyes with her coat sleeve.

Robbie sits down. He leans back on the bench and rubs his forehead with his palm.

'Sorry,' he says. 'I didn't mean to get angry. I didn't mean to swear.'

Nell sniffs. 'Tha-that's okay.'

They both stare straight ahead, at the pond and the island where a few ducks sit huddled together trying to keep warm. Nell feels exhausted. She wonders how long she could sit here before being told to move. Perhaps she could sit here until it grows dark. Perhaps she could sit here forever. She will wither away slowly until all that will be left of her will be a pile of clothes and bones.

Robbie turns to Nell. 'Let's go in and get it. I'll come with you.'

'No. I have to get a prescription from a doctor. It's Saturday. She told me to go to the hospital.'

Robbie is thoughtful. 'Then we'll go to the hospital. We'll take the bus from town. There's one that goes straight there. It takes about half an hour. I've been with my granddad.'

Nell doesn't understand why Robbie is helping her. 'Don't you need to get back? Your granddad—'

'He's fishing. He'll be out all day. I was just going to get him a packet of Rennies for his heartburn but it can wait. There are probably some in the back of the drawer anyway.' Robbie stands. 'Come on Nell. Let's get you sorted.'

Nell stands too. Her legs are shaky. She feels so tired.

'This way,' Robbie says patiently.

In the doctor's office, Robbie does most of the talking. This was what they had discussed on the bus. They would pretend to be boyfriend and girlfriend, which had been Robbie's idea.

'We'll just say we had an accident with the condom.'

'What if he doesn't give it us?'

'He'll definitely give it to us.'

Nell is worried about the doctor calling Alice. He must have all her details. What if he says he needs Alice's permission first? 'But we're both underage,' she'd told Robbie. 'What if we get into trouble? What if *you* get into trouble?'

'He's a doctor not a police officer,' Robbie had said.

It had gone exactly the way Robbie said it would. They had walked into the room holding hands, 'for effect', Robbie told her. Nell felt safer, holding Robbie's hand. She'd wondered if Robbie had wanted to hold her hand, if he would enjoy pretending to be her boyfriend. 'Don't worry,' he'd said grinning at her, reading her mind. 'I wouldn't want to be your real boyfriend. It's not that you aren't great,' he added quickly. 'I think you are. Really great. It's just that I wouldn't want to be that.'

'It's okay,' Nell had said.

The hand-holding worked. The doctor listened to Robbie explain about 'the accident' then printed the prescription, telling Nell that she should try not to be sick otherwise the pill wouldn't work, and that her period might arrive early. He told them in a matter-of-fact tone where they could get free condoms and about the benefits and drawbacks of the contraceptive pill. He explained that the morning after pill is thought to be around eighty-seven per cent effective and that Nell should take it as soon as they collect it from the pharmacy. *Eighty-seven per cent.* Her chest tightened and she felt Robbie increase the grip on her hand. They sat on the hard hospital chairs, nodding when appropriate until the doctor handed them the printed prescription. Robbie forgot to hold her hand on the way out but Nell supposed it didn't matter now that they had got what they came for.

They walked out of the revolving hospital doors towards the bus stop, Nell clutching the folded piece of paper in her pocket, Robbie walking close to Nell, wearing his grey bobble hat and coat with the worn, shiny patches.

Nell wasn't going to be pregnant. She was sure of it now. Her belly wouldn't swell and there would be no baby for Darren to drown in the water butt.

On the bus, Robbie turns to her. 'Will you see Darren again?' he asks, quietly.

'I don't know.' Nell looks into her lap. 'I don't think he would want to see me again.'

'I wouldn't bet on that,' Robbie says.

'I won't see him again,' Nell says firmly. 'I don't want to.'

227

Robbie nods.

'Why do you work for his dad then? If you hate him so much?'

Robbie presses his elbows into his knees. 'It pays more than a paper round. I suppose I don't hate him. I just don't think he's a decent person. He doesn't feel anything, you know. And I don't like how he is with girls. He was seeing this girl last year, Lucy, I think. She went to the girls' school.'

Nell glances at Robbie, letting him know it's okay for him to carry on.

'He met her at the sports centre. She played badminton or something.' Robbie coughs. 'I don't know what happened, really. All I know is she had to have time off school.'

'She was pregnant?' Nell asks, thinking of how Darren had been so angry about the condom, how his face had darkened and his voice had changed.

'There were rumours.'

'Oh,' Nell says, pushing her feet against the seat in front of her.

'I don't know for sure though,' Robbie says quickly.

They sit together in silence. Nell can feel the heavy rhythm of the wheel under her seat. Now that she has her prescription the world is less blurry, more concrete. She tries to breath deeply. 'What are you going to do after school?' she asks Robbie.

'What on Monday?'

'No,' Nell says. 'I mean, after you finish school.'

Robbie doesn't say anything and Nell wonders if he didn't hear her or if she has upset him. He blinks and scratches at the side of his face. 'I'd like to act. On the stage, or in films. It's silly, really.'

Nell looks at him. 'No, it isn't.'

'I want to earn enough to get to drama school. I've got a plan. I'll work for a couple of years first, to earn some money. I'll organise activities for kids on holiday. Go to one of those islands. I've seen them on TV. Ibiza, or somewhere like that. They have people that organise stuff, you know, water polo, discos. Not that I've ever played water polo but it can't be hard, can it?' Robbie looks at Nell and Nell feels a rush of compassion for skinny, awkward Robbie Lock who pretended to be her boyfriend and gave up his Saturday to help her.

'No,' she says. 'It can't be that hard.'

'You can live on the resorts and you get time off to go to the beach,' he tells her. 'I'll be able to save for drama school then, and get a free holiday while I'm at it.'

'I think that sounds like a good plan,' Nell says.

'Yeah.' Robbie leans back in his seat. 'I like the thought of being on an island. Surrounded by the sea.'

'But we live on an island.'

Robbie grins at her. 'Oh, yeah,' he says, 'I forget about

that.' He gestures towards the window. 'Sky's always grey though.'

Nell laughs. The sound of her laughter surprises her, as if it has come from someone else.

When they get off the bus, Robbie asks if Nell wants him to come into the pharmacy with her.

'We should make it,' he tells her, 'if we go now. They close in fifteen minutes.'

Nell shakes her head. 'I'm fine,' she says. 'I can do it by myself. Thank you though,' she adds.

Robbie shrugs. 'That's okay. See you Monday, yeah?'

Nell nods. 'See you Monday,' she echoes. She watches Robbie as he walks across the green, his hands in his pockets, his head down. The ducks are still huddled in the middle of the pond. Patches of snow remain on the green. The leaves on the weeping willow are thin and crispy, like strips of brown paper. The bench is empty. Nell crosses the road to the pharmacy, her prescription safe in her pocket.

On Sunday morning, Nell sits at the table staring at her cold toast. She wonders if she'll have to wait until her next period to find out if the pill worked. How will she be able to wait that long?

Alice enters the kitchen in her dressing gown and fills the kettle. Whilst the kettle is boiling she pours away the remains of yesterday's coffee and rinses the French press. She is wearing slippers but the backs of her ankles are bare. Nell can see several light-brown hairs on Alice's calves. She feels irritated by this. Why doesn't Alice shave her legs more often?

Nell's hair is thicker and darker than Alice's. She feels that this is a deficiency. She must have gotten the bad genes, the ugly genes, the ones Alice wants nothing to do with.

'Are you okay? You look pale.'

Nell looks up. Alice is drying the French press with a tea towel, staring at Nell.

'I'm fine.' Her voice cracks. She has an urge then, to tell Alice everything, about how mean the girls are being at school, about Darren, how she doesn't know how it happened, how ashamed she feels. She can't though. She couldn't bear Alice's disappointment.

Alice walks over and places a hand on Nell's forehead. 'You don't have a temperature.'

'I said I'm fine,' she says, her voice clearer. Nell wishes Alice wouldn't talk to her like this, like she is a child.

'Did you have a nice time in town yesterday? I forgot to ask. You rushed off again.'

'It was fine.' Nell pushes her plate away, done with her toast.

'I hope you're not coming down with something,' Alice says, peering closely at Nell.

Nell looks at the stack of art books on the table. She knows Alice bought most of her books when she was studying art. Nell sometimes thinks of Alice at art college in London. In the image in her mind, Alice, a younger Alice, is standing in front of an easel, in a large room with high windows. There is a circle of students, perhaps painting a nude. Alice will have been one of the best pupils, Nell is sure of this. She thinks of Alice graduating from university, like the students do in the films she's watched where they throw their hats into the air. Only Alice didn't graduate, Nell remembers. She left because she was pregnant.

Nell watches Alice scoop fresh coffee into the French press. She wonders if Alice hadn't got pregnant, if she might have gone to America with her father. It would have been easier with only two of them. If her father had had a good job and was married to Alice, surely Alice could have gone too? Perhaps Alice might have been happier in America. Nell pictures Alice like the American mothers she sees on TV. Alice's hair would be longer, her teeth whiter. They'd live in a blue house with a swing seat on the porch. And what if Alice had graduated from university? It might have made a difference. It might have made her more successful. Or she would have been able to teach art at a proper university instead of in the cottage kitchen, or at the local community centre.

Alice tucks a strand of loose hair behind her ear as

232

she waits for the kettle to boil. The wind blows down the cottage chimney making its whistling sound.

'It's windy this morning,' Alice says.

Nell stares at her abandoned toast. She reminds herself that she mustn't be sick.

25

On Thursday, Nell sits in her maths lesson, her legs tightly crossed. Mr Durham points to the numbers on the whiteboard with his marker pen but Nell is unable to focus on what he is saying. She looks out of the window and across the fields. She feels like she did when she used to spin herself around in the garden, when the world became soft and blurry and she wasn't sure which way she was facing or whether the green smudges in front of her eyes belonged to the grass or the trees.

All week, Nell finds she is only able to concentrate on one small task at a time. She has to tell herself to do each small task. *Put your key in your locker. Take out your science textbook. Eat half of your sandwich.* She sits at the back of the sports hall alone at lunchtime but Darren does not appear. She avoids Robbie, even when he tries to catch her eye. Despite her gratitude, Robbie reminds her how ashamed she is of herself. She doesn't want anyone to look at her, speak to her. She feels like a ghost, a paler, insipid version of herself. It's like a part of her is missing.

In the afternoon, during French, she asks to go to the bathroom, something she never usually does as she finds it embarrassing. She has to get out of the stifling classroom, even if just for five minutes.

The toilets smell of cheap hair spray and stale smoke. Nell shuts herself into one of the cubicles and leans against the door, closing her eyes, allowing herself a moment in which no effort is required to behave like a normal person. After a few seconds she hears the outside door open and someone enters the cubicle next to her. Nell flushes the toilet, pretending she has used it, then slides the lock open. She washes her hands and pulls at the towel dispenser until a clean section clicks into place. She looks at her reflection in the mirror. She is small and pale and there are circles under her eyes where she hasn't been sleeping well. A few strands of hair have escaped her bun and she tries to poke them back in.

Isobel Clayton emerges from the cubicle behind her, stopping when she sees Nell. 'Oh,' she says. The two girls stare at each other in the mirror. Isobel is the first to turn away, moving to the hand basin furthest from Nell. Nell is about to leave when Isobel speaks.

'Everyone knows you're shagging Darren Kingsley.'

'So what if I am?' Nell replies.

'So everyone knows you're a slut.'

Nell feels a familiar flush of anger. Her body stiffens.

Sensing this, Isobel takes a step back. 'You hit me again and I'll make sure you're expelled this time,' she says.

'You're not worth hitting,' Nell mutters, turning to leave.

Isobel pulls at the towel dispenser, causing it to clunk. 'Carly and I were talking about you with my mum last night.'

Nell hesitates.

'Yeah, we were telling her that everyone knows you're shagging Darren. Well, everyone except *your* mum.' Isobel smiles and Nell feels a tightening in her stomach at the mention of Alice. 'Anyway,' Isobel continues, 'my mum says it's a shame you've gone astray because you used to be a nice girl, but that we shouldn't be surprised because of your background and everything. We should feel sorry for you, really.'

'What background?' Nell's throat is dry.

'You know, with you not having a dad and with your mum not having a proper job and everything.'

'I have a dad,' Nell says.

'Oh, yeah.' Isobel smiles to herself. 'In *America*.' She lets go of the towel dispenser and stands facing Nell. 'So when did you last visit him? When was the last time he even sent you a birthday card?'

Nell opens her mouth to speak but finds she has no words.

Isobel stands grinning at her.

'Alice didn't steal that money.'

Isobel shrugs but says nothing.

'You can admit it,' Nell says. 'You can admit it to me now.'

Isobel sighs and looks warily at Nell. 'So what if I did? No one is going to believe you over me. No one is going to believe that *I* would steal something I don't need, whereas your mother could probably feed you for a year on fifty quid.'

Nell steps towards Isobel.

'Come on, Nell, hit me. Let me get you expelled. Then you'll always be like Alice. I bet Darren will get you up the duff too, if you're not already.' Isobel laughs. 'He'll fuck off and then you'll be a teenage mother, *just* like she was.'

Nell stares at Isobel. She wants to tell her that Alice was twenty-one by the time Nell was born and that Alice *does* work. Instead, she turns around and walks out the door.

When Nell arrives home from school, Alice is out. There is a letter addressed to Nell on the doormat, along with a large envelope for Alice. Nell knows that her letter is from Rachel because she recognises the familiar rounded handwriting. Nell has not heard from Rachel for several months. Last summer they had talked about trying to meet up but the logistics seemed too complicated. *Never mind*, Rachel had written. *We can meet up when our parents will let us travel on the train by ourselves.* Nell had felt there was a distance to Rachel's last letter. It was full of her friends and her life in Devon and, apart from the comment about them travelling on the train by themselves, it felt more like a diary entry, a list of recent events, than a letter written to a best friend.

Nell sits down on the sofa, still in her coat. She opens the letter and begins to read. Rachel has included a photograph of herself with Minnie Mouse at Disneyland Paris. She tells Nell she went there during the February half term. *I want to tell you something but it's top secret,* Rachel writes. *I have a boyfriend! His name is Thomas Andrew Jeffries and he lives near me but goes to a boys' school. We met at the stables. Last weekend he took me to the cinema and put his arm around me. I think it was very uncomfortable for him because at the end of the film he kept swinging his arm as if his shoulder had gone stiff. Then on Wednesday we took his dogs for a walk. He's got two golden retrievers, Freddie and Beatrice (both girls). He opened every gate for me so I could go through first and he helped me down off the stile by offering me his hand. After that we held hands all the way back until we reached the main road. On Sunday evening he came over to mine for dinner. My dad made a chicken curry but Thomas was so nervous he couldn't eat. My dad kept asking him if he was okay and if the chicken was too spicy for him. After dinner I showed him my room whilst my parents were in the living room watching*

TV. We sat on my bed and talked about how much we both
liked each other and then we kissed! I don't think either of us
knew what we were supposed to do or what it was supposed
to be like but it was very nice! He kept asking me if I was
okay and telling me he liked me. He said it over and over
again as if he couldn't say anything else. 'I really like you
Rachel. I really, really like you.' I giggled a little bit because it
was like the words were falling out of his mouth and he had
no control over them. After that he inflated my blow-up chair
with his bicycle pump, then he went home. My mum really
likes him because he's good at quizzes. He wants to go on
University Challenge one day. Have you kissed a boy, Nell?
It doesn't matter if you haven't. A lot of my friends haven't
yet and I don't think I would have done if I hadn't met
Thomas, I just wondered because you've never mentioned it.
Has Alice bought a computer yet?

Love
Rachel (and Clover)

Nell puts the letter down. She thinks of Darren, of the
Doritos and the guns and the bloodstain on his sheet. She
thinks of her fight with Isobel Clayton and the girls at
school who all know she's a slut. Rachel is normal and
Nell is not. Darren Kingsley would never go for a walk
with her and hold her hand or come over to the cottage
for dinner. Even if he did, Alice would not talk to him
about quiz shows.

239

Nell screws the letter up and walks back into the hallway. She puts her shoes on and lets herself out of the front door. She throws the letter in the wheelie bin.

Nell will not write back to Rachel. She doesn't know what to say or how to answer her question about if she's ever kissed a boy. Rachel's life is now a world away from Nell's.

In her room, she takes the piece of paper with Rachel's address on from the drawer next to her bed and takes it into the bathroom where she burns it in the sink with her lighter. She rinses the ash away and dries her hands. Rachel is better off without a friend like her. Rachel deserves better.

Downstairs, Nell hears Alice enter the cottage, the sound of her throwing her keys into the green bowl. A few minutes later, Alice is calling her.

'Nell,' Alice shouts up the stairs. 'Come and have a look at this.'

Nell goes downstairs.

Alice hands her a flyer. 'It's for my exhibition in Lincoln next month.'

Nell takes the flyer from Alice. *The Return of Alice Mae.*

Return from what? Nell wonders.

A prominent portrait artist in the mid nineteen eighties, Mae is a realist painter known for her expressionistic use of line and colour. Her portraits offer an uncanny and often intense psychological insight into her subject matter. Mae depicts the basic facts of life in her startling portraits and unashamed female nudes. She captures both the dignity and the vulnerability of her subjects.

'So you're going to be famous again,' Nell says.

'It's only a small gallery in Lincoln,' Alice replies. 'Hardly the Tate.'

Nell puts the flyer next to the utensil pot. She wants to go to her room but Alice is already warming something on the hob she must have cooked earlier. She reaches into the cupboard for bowls which means dinner will be ready soon. Nell knows she should offer to help lay the table, or fill their glasses with water but she doesn't feel she has the energy. She sits at the kitchen table and stares at the salt and pepper pots.

'Try not to scratch,' Alice says.

Irritated, Nell pulls her hand out of her jumper arm.

'How is your skin?' Alice asks.

'The same.'

The saucepan has begun to bubble. Alice turns it off. Nell can smell spices: turmeric, garlic and cumin. She wonders what Isobel Clayton is having for dinner, then she wonders what her father in California is having for dinner. She watches Alice reaching for the ladle and recalls the look on Isobel's face when she'd mentioned her father, that smirk. *When was the last time he sent you a birthday card?*

She wonders, now, why it had been enough to simply

imagine her father, to know he was out there living his life in America, without needing to know more.

'I want to ask you something.'

'Mm?' Alice is spooning stew evenly into two bowls.

Nell takes a deep breath. 'I just want to know whereabouts in America my father is.'

Alice puts the ladle slowly down on the chopping board and turns to face Nell, her expression blank. 'America?'

Nell takes a deep breath. 'I know he isn't coming back. I only want to know where he is.'

Alice puts the steaming bowls on the table.

'I thought maybe California?' Nell says. 'It doesn't matter. It's just... people ask, you know.'

Alice blinks. 'Why do you think he's in America?'

'Because that's what you said.'

'When?'

'I asked you in the doctor's waiting room and you pointed to the map. Then Mike... remember your friend Mike?'

Alice nods. She has one hand on the back of the kitchen chair.

'Well, Mike gave me that book on California...' Nell trails off because Alice's expression has not changed.

'I don't remember that,' Alice says finally. 'I don't remember telling you he was in America.'

Nell can feel her insides turning cold.

Alice pulls her chair back. 'You used to ask me sometimes when you were little, why you didn't have a dad. I guess I tried to give you answers I thought might help.' She runs a hand through her hair then sits down.

Nell sits too. Her body feels like a block of ice. She picks up her spoon, her hand shaky. *Act normal. Don't let her see you're upset about this* 'Where is he then?' She asks the question casually, as if it is of little interest to her, 'if he isn't in America?'

Alice eats a small spoonful of stew. 'I've no idea. I couldn't care less, I'm afraid.' She pauses, her spoon half way to her mouth. 'But I am sorry, if you thought he was in America.'

Nell shrugs. The gesture is hard work. She looks at a small brown stain on the tablecloth. 'It doesn't really matter. It was just something I thought.'

Alice eats slowly. 'This is good,' she says. 'The best one I've done for a while. There's quite a lot of garlic.'

Nell looks around the small kitchen, at the faded patch of lino by the oven, the washing up on the draining board, the thin chequered curtains. It is only six o'clock but it's already dark. Nell can see their reflections in the window, her and Alice sitting opposite each other at the table. She has the sudden realisation that this is all there is. Her father, in California, does not exist. There is only

243

this dark February evening and tomorrow, a slow walk across muddy fields, cold classrooms, the girls who don't like her, and Darren who had sex with her. Her life is no different to anyone else's and she hates herself for ever thinking it might be.

Part Five

26

2005

Four and a half hours later, Nell is climbing out of a taxi outside the cottage. The dykes are high with spring rain and the cows are in the fields. Alice has painted the front door yellow. Other than the door, the cottage looks the same. There are the familiar square windows, terracotta roof tiles and red brick chimney with its two black chimney pots. The taxi drives away and Nell opens the gate. The front garden is overgrown, just the way Alice likes it. Nell remembers a man knocking on the door once and offering to mow and tidy the front garden. 'I could make it really nice for you,' he had said.

'We like it like this,' Alice had explained. 'It's better for the insects.'

Above the front window there is a tangle of wisteria branches. They creep up and around the right side of the cottage. Already Nell can see several tiny buds. On the front step sits a pot full of chives. Nell brushes her fingers against them. She takes her keys from inside her rucksack and slowly opens the door.

Inside, nothing has changed. There is the small green bowl on the hall table where Alice keeps her keys. Several canvases rest against the opposite wall. There are two pairs of wellies, hers and Alice's, and a red umbrella. Nell steps into the living room, onto the long bare floorboards with their familiar knots and grooves.

Alice is descending the stairs. She stops when she sees Nell. 'Oh.' And when Nell turns her face, 'Oh, my God.' Alice hurries down the stairs. She rushes forward and hugs Nell.

Nell allows herself to be hugged, then slowly frees herself from Alice's embrace. She sits on the sofa and begins to take her trainers off. Alice stands watching as if, if she moves, Nell might disappear.

Nell sinks back into the sofa, closing her eyes.

'Would you like a cup of tea?'

Nell nods without opening her eyes. There is the familiar sound of Alice in the kitchen, the sound of the kettle and of the kitchen cupboard opening and closing.

Nell finally opens her eyes as Alice returns with two steaming mugs which she places on the coffee table.

'I'll make you something to eat,' Alice says. 'Whatever you want.'

Nell hasn't eaten all day but she has no idea what she wants to eat. The question, the decision, is too difficult, and so she says nothing.

Alice keeps looking at her. 'Has this happened before?'

Alice is looking at her eye, her bandaged wrist. Nell isn't sure. Has this happened before? She has had a black eye before so she supposes it has.

'Yes,' she says.

Alice looks into her mug. 'I'm glad you're here,' she says quietly. 'If I ever see him again, I'll kill him.'

Nell nods and they drink their tea in silence.

Nell doesn't leave the cottage for over a week. She eats small meals, whatever Alice brings her. She sleeps a lot during the day and then finds she is also able to sleep at night. Alice asks to photograph Nell. 'Just in case,' Alice says.

Nell knows what Alice means. *Just in case we need to show someone what that man did to you.*

Nell doesn't care about that, but if Alice wants to take her photograph, she doesn't mind. She understands. 'Take me how you want.'

'Are you sure?' Alice asks, surprised.

And so they spend several afternoons, whilst Nell's eye is still bruised, setting up and shooting in the garden until Alice is happy she has something.

After two weeks at the cottage, Nell begins to sleep less during the day, although she is still unable to cope with anything that requires even the smallest amount of concentration. She completes menial household chores, even though Alice tells her not to bother. She sweeps the floors, cleans the kitchen and bathroom, hangs the washing out then spends time folding it carefully. It is April, sunny and dry. Nell wanders around the garden, holding a cup of tea. She likes the mornings best when the grass is still slightly damp and she can listen to the birds: the blue tits, sparrows, chaffinches and blackbirds singing their chorus. Alice has made a wildflower garden in the area of long grass by the shed and the plum tree. 'For the bees,' she had said.

Each morning Nell inspects the new wildflower area. She watches the bluebells grow. She likes their shape, their elegant curve. She remembers Grandma telling her that fairies use the bluebells to catch unwanted passers-by. There are not only bluebells in Alice's small patch of wild garden but cowslip, and one or two pink dog rose flowers. Nell looks at the new white buds on the plum tree. Perhaps, she thinks, this is what my life will be like from now on. I will spend each day doing nothing but watching the tiny gestures of small flowers.

She begins to read again, taking books from the cottage bookshelf, curling up with them on the flowery armchair. Losing herself in other times and other worlds somehow manages to bring Nell slowly back to herself.

After almost three weeks, she feels ready to leave the cottage. They drive to the coast and walk along the deserted beach in their wellies. At first, Nell is anxious.

She thinks that perhaps, out of the cottage, Alice will ask her the questions she doesn't want to answer. But Alice doesn't ask. She only walks with Nell, stopping and bending down every now and then to examine a shell or a stone.

One afternoon, when they return from the beach, she catches her reflection in the hallway mirror. She touches her cheek. It's as if there is a little more of herself there. Not everything. Not yet. But something more than just an outline. The colour is returning to her cheeks. She no longer has to pinch herself to make sure she is there. She is filling herself in.

One night, after they have both gone to bed, Nell hears the sound of a car stopping outside the cottage. She sits up and switches the light on. There are footsteps, someone crunching up the gravel path. The gait is familiar. She holds her breath, her heart racing. She forces herself to get out of bed, throwing her dressing gown on over her pyjamas, and steps onto the landing where she bumps into Alice.

'It's him,' Nell whispers, backing up against the wall.

Alice holds Nell's shoulders. 'Don't panic,' she says, firmly. 'It could be anything. I'll have a look.'

Nell stands in the doorway of Alice's bedroom and watches as Alice gingerly pulls the curtain back. Nell can see only the dark night sky, the thinnest slice of moon, but Alice looks down. She closes the curtain quickly and turns to Nell. 'A black car.'

Nell tries to speak but her throat is tight and dry. She stands, rooted to the spot. She knows it's him.

'I should call the police,' Alice says.

Nell thinks about how much trouble she'll be in with Scott if she calls the police. *You little bitch*, he'll say. *My own girlfriend!* She shakes her head, whispers, 'No. If we don't answer the door, he'll just go away.' As she speaks the words out loud, she knows they aren't true. Scott won't give up. He has driven all this way, determined. She knows he won't leave without her.

Alice steps past Nell onto the landing. 'I don't care, I'm calling the police.'

There's a loud knock at the door and they both freeze.

Alice shoots Nell a worried glance. 'My mobile's downstairs.'

There is another knock and then Scott's voice.

'Nell, I know you're there,' Scott shouts. 'Nell!' He pounds on the front door. They can hear the plant pot breaking. She wonders how Scott found her. Did he go to Teresa? Charm her into giving him Alice's address somehow? She must have put Alice down as her next of kin when she first started the job. Or did she leave her address lying around in Scott's flat? Why has it taken him almost a month? *Because he thought I'd come back. He can't believe he's really lost me.* Nell realises that Scott *has* to get her back, that to lose her would be more than he could bear.

The knocking and banging stops. Everything goes quiet. Alice and Nell look at each other. 'Perhaps he's leaving,' Nell whispers.

Alice tiptoes across the room and over to the window. 'He's going around the back.'

'Did you lock the door?'

'I don't know.' Alice turns to Nell. 'If he gets in, we'll tell him *calmly* to leave. We'll say we've already called the police.'

Nell follows Alice onto the landing. They wait at the top of the stairs. Nell is trembling so badly her teeth are chattering. She presses her arms into her sides. Alice puts her hand on Nell's shoulder.

There is a click, the sound of the back door opening. They can hear footsteps in the kitchen. Neither of them remembered to lock the back door. They often don't. The farmer's house is half a mile away. There's nothing else around. Just fields.

'Nell. I know you're here.' Scott's voice sounds close, his speech slightly slurred. They can hear him moving through the kitchen, then crashing about in the living room.

He appears at the bottom of the stairs. 'Nell,' he says, looking up at her, his eyes wide and damp, his pupils dilated.

Alice puts her arm protectively around Nell. 'I want you to leave,' she tells Scott. 'We've called the police.'

Scott laughs cruelly and Nell shivers. His expression changes and he looks mournfully at Nell. 'You know I love you, Nell.'

Nell says nothing. She can't stop shaking.

'I want you to leave *now*,' Alice repeats.

Scott steps onto the bottom stair. He puts one hand against the wall to steady himself.

'Don't come any further,' Alice warns him.

Scott stops. He wipes his hand across his forehead. 'Come on Nell. You know she's crazy. She's never done anything for you. Not one single fucking thing. What are you going to do without me?'

Nell closes her eyes. She doesn't want to look at Scott's face, at his pleading eyes. Her breath seems to be bursting out of her chest, quick and shallow. Her fists are tightly clenched. When she opens her eyes, Scott is still looking at her.

'It's killing me,' he says, 'being apart from you. We're made for each other, Nell. We're supposed to be together, remember? Come home with me.' He puts his hand out. 'Come with me now and we'll forget all about this.'

'She's not going anywhere,' Alice says coolly.

'I couldn't stand it,' Scott says, 'if I couldn't be with you. I'd marry you tomorrow, Nell, I really would.' He takes another step.

Nell shrinks back against the wall. She can feel the blood pumping through her ears.

'We're not listening to your bullshit,' Alice says.

Scott looks up. His eyes flash with anger. He takes two more steps up the stairs. 'I wasn't talking to you, bitch.'

'Get out of my house,' Alice shouts. 'I'm warning you, the police will be here any minute.' Scott's face darkens. 'Give her to me,' he says, taking another step.

'Don't be ridiculous. You don't *own* her,' Alice hisses.

Scott reaches the top of the stairs. He lunges forward. Nell screams and then Scott is falling backwards. Alice has pushed him. Her weight is no match for Scott's but he has lost his footing on the steep staircase. He slips on the foot that is not his own. There is a horrible noise as Scott's skull hits the tiles. His body is twisted awkwardly at the waist.

Nell and Alice remain at the top of the stairs holding onto each other. They wait for Scott to get up but he doesn't move. Blood, dark and sticky, pools around his head. His eyes are open, unblinking. Nell stares at Scott. She looks into his blank brown eyes, the eyes that have looked at her so many times before in anger, in disgust. As she looks at Scott's eyes they change colour, from brown to grey. In Scott's eyes she now also sees the dead, expressionless eyes of Darren Kingsley.

They seem to sit there, clinging tightly to each other, for a long time, but in fact, it is probably only several minutes. Eventually, Alice lets go of Nell and Nell watches as Alice creeps down the stairs towards Scott.

'I-I don't think you should touch him,' Nell calls weakly to Alice. 'We need to call an ambulance.'

Ignoring her, Alice leans over Scott, watching him carefully, as if he might at any moment jump up. She places two fingers on his neck and leaves them there for several long seconds.

'He's dead,' she says.

Alice climbs back up the stairs, to where Nell is crouching next to the storage heater on the landing. Alice slumps down opposite Nell. It's quiet, still. Somewhere, outside the cottage, in the black spring night, an owl hoots.

It's Nell who speaks first. 'He fell,' she whispers to Alice. 'He was running up the stairs and he fell.'

Alice nods. She gets up and slowly goes back downstairs. She tiptoes around Scott and picks up her phone from the kitchen worktop. She calls for an ambulance. The nearest hospital is over forty-five minutes away but a first responder on a motorbike arrives fifteen minutes after Alice's call. He does all he can. It is the paramedics who pronounce Scott dead.

In the days following Scott's death, Alice kept asking Nell if she was okay and Nell kept thinking she should be asking Alice the same question. Although shocked, Nell did, in fact, feel surprisingly okay. It was such an awful thing to have happened and yet she felt strangely calm, and free.

High amounts of alcohol were found in Scott's blood. A detective had appeared at the cottage three days after the accident and Nell and Alice had taken him through exactly what had happened, how Scott had arrived drunk, broken in and tripped on the steep and unfamiliar staircase. 'My mother had a similar accident on these stairs. Over ten years ago now. They thought she might have been rushing to get to the telephone. She used to wear these slippers with no backs...'

'God, I'm so sorry, Alice,' the detective had said, after writing something down in his tiny notepad.

The detective had been at school with Alice. A short, balding man with scuffed shoes, he'd stood at the bottom of the stairs, holding the cup of tea Alice made for him and shaking his head. 'A terrible thing,' he'd said. 'Treacherous, these old staircases. Even if you've got two legs.'

'It's really been so awful. It's so good of you to come out, Rupert. And so good to see you. Do you still play the violin?'

The detective glanced bashfully at Alice. 'Ha, no. Goodness, I'm surprised you remember the violin. I was bloody awful. The screecher, my dad used to call it.'

'I thought you were good.'

257

The detective blushed and drained the last of his tea. 'Bloody good tea this, Alice.'

'Thank you, Alice had said, flashing him a smile, offering to take his mug.

27

She walks through Covent Garden wearing her parka, a hat, gloves and scarf. It's the first week in December and the air is sharp and cold on her face yet she feels warm because she is walking, and because she has just come from the Underground. She passes a Christmas tree with pink and white lights where tourists are taking photographs. The shops all have their Christmas windows in. She can smell roasting chestnuts from a nearby stall. The pavements are beginning to frost and she can see her breath in front of her face as she walks. She smiles to herself, enjoying the city, the moment. Both London and the evening belong to her.

Nell can't believe she has completed a whole term at university already. It's gone so quickly, a flurry of lectures, seminars, of standing in the courtyard with her classmates drinking tea from paper cups whilst talking about their favourite writers or else speculating about the interests and motivations of their tutors. And then, of course, there has been the reading. So much reading. Nell spends her evenings sitting on the bed in her studio apartment with a book, or at the small desk working on her laptop. She no longer has to hide her books under the bed, which is a good thing because she has many. She crosses the road and heads towards Seven Dials wondering if Alice is already at the gallery.

Nell has not seen Alice since Alice's first visit to London in October. Nell had left the cottage for London early in September after spending almost seven months at home in Lincolnshire.

During those months at the cottage, Nell hadn't known where to go, only that she must do something, go somewhere. She had not expected to get a place at university, despite an excellent reference from Mrs Williams, her old English teacher. She had left it late to apply— it was already April. And she had no A levels meaning she would not have the required UCAS points. Of the four universities she had applied for, three had rejected her. The first, within a matter of days. When Nell received the rejection from the third, she rang their admissions department. The woman on the other end of the phone had told her she would never get a place without A-levels. She suggested Nell take an access course, try again in a year. Nell hadn't wanted to wait a year. She'd found an email address for the course leader at the one remaining university, explained that she would be grateful for a place, that she intended to work hard. The course leader, a woman named Naomi Abyoie, asked Nell to send in two samples of her work, an essay and a creative piece, as she had applied for joint honours in

English Literature and Creative Writing. Nell had looked at Naomi Abyoie's profile on the university website: she had studied English at Stanford, completed her MFA in Creative Writing in Iowa and had a PhD in African-American Literature. Her publications included a novel called *Green Swan Crying* that had been long-listed for the women's prize for fiction five years ago. Nell had sighed. She'd never even had a short story published, and the last essay she wrote was for her English GCSE. She had notebooks filled with stories and poems but were they any good? She'd stayed up into the early hours of the morning writing about the issues of class in *Howard's End*, and a short story about a man who sees a woman, an old flame, at a friend's funeral. She emailed the pieces to Naomi and, the following week, received an unconditional offer. Now here she is, one term through already.

Alice had visited six weeks after Nell moved to London. She'd opened cupboards, peered inside the fridge, told Nell that, already, she had a container of olives at the back that were 'floating in fluff'.

Nell didn't think she could face living with someone after Scott, even flatmates. She wasn't ready. She'd taken a weekend job in a jewellery shop and another, two nights a week, waitressing in a Turkish restaurant with blue walls. The badly-paid jobs supplemented her student loan and she'd been able to afford the studio room. She had a bed, a desk, a chair and a wardrobe. The kitchen consisted of a sink with one cupboard below it and another above. There was a microwave oven fixed to the wall. The building had once been a textile factory and the flat's one redeeming feature was that the window in her room was huge. She liked to sit on the deep windowsill in the evenings looking out at the never-quite-dark London sky. She was so close to the building next to hers she could hear the neighbours' shower running at seven thirty every morning; their Velux window would be open to let the steam out.

Nell has been so busy these three months, she sometimes lets things get out of hand. Wispy dust balls drift across the floor. The bathroom mirror is specked and misty, the shower frequently blocked with hair. Coffee cup rings accumulate on the wooden desk. Cardboard packaging and empty water bottles stand by the door, Nell never having a spare five minutes to do the recycling. Her book towers are already growing like triffids from the floor. She puts some on the windowsill but they keep getting wet. The books fatten and swell, the pages drying out and becoming crispy. The spines are faded from the winter sun.

Alice had asked Nell, that visit, if she'd made any friends. Nell had said yes. She'd thought of Louie, Art, Dylan, and Lexi. She'd known they were her group, the joint honours group, as soon as she'd seen them, as soon they'd shuffled out of the induction seminar and along the corridor, reaching into their pockets for roll-ups and zippo lighters. Dylan was from Cornwall. Big and bearded, there was something caveman about him. Louie was from Manchester. He wore a huge shearling coat with badges and heavy boots. Art was skinny and his eye twitched when he was nervous. He wore flowery blouses, medallions and a black pork pie hat. Lexi was in a short leather skirt, platform boots and thick black eyeliner.

Nell had been terrified that first day. She'd expected all the others to have come straight from their A-levels. She needn't have worried. Dylan had taken a year out due to his mental health. Lexi had spent her first year after school working in bars and her second travelling. Louie was the same age as Nell, having worked for his dad's company for a while. Only Art had come straight from his A-levels. All the hours she had spent reading as escapism suddenly appeared to add up and become useful. They all wanted to be writers, although none of them quite knew what being a writer would involve other than working menial jobs, living in dingy accommodation, and accumulating student debt. Nell had talked about her new friends and Alice listened. They'd taken the bus to Camden then walked to Primrose Hill. The day was cloudy, not the best for the view. Once they'd reached the top Alice had sat on the bench, held her rucksack on her knees and taken in the city. Nell wondered if Alice would pull out her sketch pad and draw the young French couple standing on the viewing platform, their arms wrapped around each other, but she hadn't.

'The skyline has changed,' Alice said.

'Yes,' Nell replied, although she didn't remember the skyline any other way.

What would London have been like when Alice first arrived? Had she felt excited? Overwhelmed? In a few weeks' time Nell would be the same age as Alice was when she became pregnant with Nell.

'I always wondered,' Nell had said, that day on Primrose Hill. 'Why you decided to have me. I guess I always sort of assumed you didn't know. That it was too late for you to do anything about it.'

Alice had glanced at Nell, touched her scarf at her throat. Her eyes quickly returned to the skyline. 'I suppose you're right. I didn't realise. Not at first.'

Nell nodded, used to Alice, her brutal truths. She had prepared herself.

'I wasn't sure what to do, really,' Alice had said, slowly. 'I hadn't thought much, at that point. I didn't want to think about it – although I suppose I knew it wasn't too late. But then I got on the tube one morning. There had been a lot of stuff in the news again, around that time, about IRA threats. It was all still going on, I suppose. I was two months pregnant, or thereabouts.' Alice had turned to look at Nell. 'I knew,' she said. 'I knew but I don't think I had allowed myself to think about it, you know?'

Nell nodded.

'So there I was, getting on the tube and then there was this bang and people were screaming. Someone had thrown something onto the train just before the doors closed. It made such a noise. Obviously, everyone thought it was a bomb. In that moment, I didn't think of me at all. I thought of you. I thought *please let my baby be okay. Please let her be alright.* I always thought of you as a girl, you know.'

Nell had looked down at her gloved hands in her lap. 'It wasn't a bomb then,' she said.

'No. Someone went and picked it up. It was a frozen chicken wrapped in a plastic bag.'

Nell looked at Alice then began to laugh. Alice laughed too. There they were, sitting on the bench on top of Primrose Hill unable to stop laughing whilst the French couple turned around and smiled at them.

'A *chicken*,' Alice said, giggling again.

Nell crosses the road and over to the gallery on the corner. She enters through the doors and sees a table with leaflets advertising the exhibition. Her face is on the front of the leaflet. The exhibition is called *Daughter*. Nell knows already that this is the name of the exhibition but still, her face on the leaflet, a close-up from one of Alice's paintings, takes her aback. Alice had rung Nell in September and told her about the exhibition. 'I'll only use the images and paintings I have your permission to use.'

Nell had thought for a moment. 'Use whatever you want,' she'd said.

She takes off her coat and hat, folds the coat over her arm, and enters the large white space of the gallery. Facing her on the wall is a painting of herself at fourteen, sitting on the edge of the bath. She's looking down whilst holding the towel tightly up to her chest. The painting is called *Child no longer*. She stares at the title, her mouth falling open. How could Alice have known?

She steps back, recovers herself. From the other side of the room, she can hear voices, chatter, the clinking of glasses. A huddle of glamourous-looking people stand next to two tables stacked with champagne glasses. Alice is with a tall man in a pinstripe suit, laughing at something. She's wearing a blue dress, red lipstick and large silver earrings. She moves easily amongst the people who all want to talk to her. She sees Nell and gives her a small wave. Nell waves back and several people follow Alice's gaze. Nell turns away. She doesn't want to be recognised as the subject of the exhibition. She had been undecided, right up until the point she left her room, as to whether to come tonight. In the end, she had felt it important, for Alice's sake. It is her opening night after all.

The exhibition has already received a lot of interest. Last weekend, there had been an article on Alice in the

Observer: Artist. Woman. Mother. Conservationist. Alice Mae is a portrait artist with a strong social conscience and a long-held interest in sustainability. Intimate and direct, Alice Mae's 'Daughter' portraits exist as an unparalleled chronicle of motherhood and the mother/daughter relationship. She is surely one of Britain's most engaging figurative painters working today. Alice had also written an article for *The Sunday Times* about the history of photography becoming art and why she had chosen the two mediums, paint and photography, for her subject.

'You could come if you want. I mean, you do *live* in London now.'

She could picture Alice sitting on the chair in the cottage, holding the phone, her red scarf in her hair.

'Of course I'll be there,' she had said.

A young man in a white shirt and black tie appears at Nell's shoulder with a tray and offers her a glass of champagne. She takes one, thanking him. The gallery is filling up, people are beginning to move around the exhibition. Nell turns the corner and finds herself looking at a portrait Alice painted of her in the London flat. She is three, maybe four. She stands with her hands on her hips, wearing nothing but knickers and a grey flat cap one of Alice's friends had given her to play with. The painting has a much less ambiguous title: *Eleonora in a hat.*

There are many more paintings of Nell as a child. In some she looks sulky, in others, precocious. Then there are two photographs Alice took the summer they moved to the cottage – Nell lying on her tummy with her fishing net on the wooden bridge over the stream. She has one leg stretched out, the other tucked underneath her. The long fishing net over the water mirrors her outstretched leg. She looks as though she might, at any minute, topple into the stream. The picture appears to be a moment captured, but in reality Alice had spent all afternoon adjusting Nell, working with the light, trying to get the angles and proportions the way she wanted them. The photograph is called *Tadpole*, perhaps because Nell is fishing for tadpoles or perhaps because, with her one outstretched leg, she looks a little like a tadpole herself.

The second photograph is of Nell in the wheat field behind the cottage. She is holding a chequered blanket over her shoulders and squinting at the camera. Alice has named the photograph *Hayfever*.

On the opposite wall there is a painting of Nell when she was sixteen. She is curled up in the cottage living room reading *Pride and Prejudice*. Alice has painted the tiny pink flowers on Grandma's armchair. Nell has her eyebrows knitted together. Her hair is pulled up on top of her head in a top-knot held together with a blue scrunchie. She's wearing a black T-shirt and frayed denim shorts. In this painting, Nell's skin has a strange greenish tinge; Alice has given it the title *Frowning at Mr Darcy*.

As Nell stands looking at the painting she has seen

so many times before, but never here, she is aware of a man next to her looking at the caption. Nell sips her champagne and makes to move away.

'I always said she could do it.'

Nell glances at the man, probably in his late sixties, maybe early seventies. He's wearing pink trousers and a cord jacket. His hair is thick and silvery and sticks out from under his hat. He's holding a glass of champagne. There is no one else within ear shot so Nell assumes he must be talking to her.

'Sorry?'

'I always knew, out of all of them, she had the potential to make it. She had real talent, Alice.' The man gives Nell a long sideways glance. 'I was her teacher.'

'Oh.' Nell doesn't remember Alice ever mentioning any of her teachers.

'I read about the exhibition in the *Independent* last week,' the man says, his eyes now firmly fixed on Nell. I haven't had a chance to speak to Alice yet. Are you a student?' He smiles and takes a step closer.

'Oh, no. I mean, yes, I am, but not an art student.'

'Oh? What's your field then?'

The man's gaze is intense.

'I'm studying English and Creative Writing.'

'Ah, a writer,' the man says. 'I'm John.' He holds his hand out.

She shakes his hand. 'Nell.'

269

'Are you here for inspiration,' he asks, 'for your writing? Or are you buying?' His eyes sparkle mischievously. He thinks she can't afford to buy one of Alice's paintings. He doesn't know she doesn't need to. Nell can smell the alcohol on his breath. Not the champagne. Something else. She takes a step back. 'Actually…' This is exactly the reason she hadn't wanted to come. 'I'm Alice's daughter.'

The man, John, glances around the gallery then back at Nell. 'It's you then,' he tells her, 'in the paintings, and the photographs. It's all you.'

'Yes.'

He looks at her now with new interest. 'It must be strange,' he says slowly, 'to see yourself here – as subject. Here is the real you, but on the walls – there is the you that people will think they see.'

Nell blinks. 'I guess it's all me.' For some reason she doesn't want to give this man, John, the satisfaction of agreeing with him. She *does* feel that the girl on the walls is now someone different to herself but then, in each piece, there is, of course, a part of her.

What Nell really sees in each painting, or photograph, is not only her, but Alice. When she was small and she used to sit for Alice, Alice would tell her they were making art together. She realises, now, what Alice meant.

John peers at the painting again then turns to her. 'I didn't know Alice had children until I saw the name of the exhibition.'

'Well, there's just me.' Nell looks around, searching for an escape. The gallery is filling up. 'I hope you enjoy the rest of the exhibition,' she says, stepping quickly away.

'Good luck then,' John calls after her, 'with your writing.'

As she turns the corner Nell sees the final painting, *Coming Home*. It's the painting Alice was working on last spring. Nell is sitting on the kitchen stool wearing leggings and a camisole. Her black eye is visible, as is the tatty bandage on her wrist. There is a bruise on her shoulder from where she hit the TV unit in Scott's flat as she fell.

She moves away from the painting, thinking of her room back in Finsbury Park waiting for her, of her books and her reading lamp. One of the waiting staff passes and she puts her empty glass on his tray. When she gets in, she will turn the heating on, make a cup of herbal tea, perhaps have a slice of toast before getting into bed with her book.

She puts her coat on and pulls her hat down low over her ears. Alice is still surrounded by people. Nell decides to slip quietly out the gallery doors, into the soft London night and crisp December air. Alice will understand.